The King of Birds

By

J. K. Zimmerman

Dedication: to Michael, for a myriad of reasons, but above all for love and inspiration

Many thanks to Luke, for being my faithful writing partner

Thanks to: Jenny, Theresa, and Diana. Special thanks to Doug and Jackie.

Thanks to all for the encouragement and support in this endeavor.

Note: This story takes place in and around Dayton, Ohio. All the places mentioned by name are real places (except Mama Wertman's) but all the characters are works of fiction.

I've been keeping a journal ever since my high school English teacher, Mrs. Merritt, pointed her bony finger at me and demanded, "You must write everyday, Jonathan Swift Somers, whether you feel like it or not!"

It is good advice for young writers. I have developed the habit of writing my in my journal every night before bed. Moreover, never one to write to an unknown audience, for the last few years I've written my diary entries to Sam Hookey—the one that got away, to be precise the one who walked away. It is from those journals that I've compiled this account.

Wednesday July 12, 2017

Dear Sam,
Today, I ran into Edmund Pollard. He hasn't changed a bit. Not that I knew him well to begin with; we only hung out a few times in the summer of 2014, he was a friend of a friend of a friend. He definitely is NOT my type, but I can't deny I'm attracted to him. God knows why, he's gaunt, pale, lacking charm, but he is damn smart. You well know I could never stand a vapid man. Not that I'm saying he is gay, my gaydar didn't ping much around him, but he didn't give off a straight vibe either—more of an asexual thing.

He said he was glad to have run into me. He wanted my help with some theory he was working on. He asked if we could meet tomorrow for coffee. I, of course, immediately agreed. I'm not sure what help I can offer him—he's a forensic accountant. He is able to dig through a company's or person's finances and find discrepancies. The police employ him mostly, but he does take on private clients too. My skills are with words, not numbers. Maybe he needs my help with writing a proposal or something. We exchanged numbers. I am eager to see what tomorrow will bring. It has been a while since I had a date, not that this is really one. But I can pretend. It is nice to be wanted, no matter what the reason.

Thursday July 13, 2017

Dear Sam,
I'm finishing my third beer of the night, it's been one of those days (now, don't say that drinking beer is a ding against my gay card, it's

an artisanal IPA I picked up from Warped Wing). I met Edmund for coffee—though we both ended up having tea. He was dressed in tan cargo pants and a wrinkled short sleeve dress shirt. Fashion awards, he will not win. We sat across a small cafe table, just watching the steam rise from our tea. I could see him trying to figure out the best way to broach the subject of his theory. Calling on all my years of journalism experience of getting people to open up, I offered, with a smile, "I'm all ears." That's all he needed to jump into his theory: he thinks that there is a serial killer operating in the city.

Okay, definitely not what I thought he was going to say. But I was intrigued and asked him why he thought so. I don't remember any word of that kind of thing on the news—not that I'm a news junkie, I've always been more of a Project Runway junkie, as you know. He said that while working with the police he overhears things and has a fair amount of freedom to read police reports. And he has identified three victims that he thinks were killed by the same person.

The first incident happened three months ago, it was a rainy April night and a man was walking along some railroad tracks. For whatever reason, he didn't hear the train or get off the tracks in time and it ran him over. He was identified as John Cabanis, a 37 year old African American male. His autopsy showed no alcohol or drugs in his system. His family stated that that night he went out for a drive which he did from time to time to clear his mind. But it was not his habit to walk the railroad tracks, especially in a thunderstorm. He was killed just three miles from his house. The train engineer stated that he saw a figure on the tracks but there is no way to stop a 15,000 ton train in any way that would have avoided the accident. The coroner ruled it an accidental death and the police did not investigate any further.

He delivered the details of this tragedy with all the cold detachment of an accountant—brrrr.

The second death happened last month to a 55 year old Caucasian woman named Amelia Garrack. She was out on her daily walk when a power line somehow came loose and came in contact with her, killing her instantly. Again, her autopsy showed no alcohol or drugs in her system. And again she was killed less then three miles from her house. The power company investigated the power line and concluded that, even though maintenance had been performed on it less than six months before, the elements must have eroded the connection and the line fell. The coroner ruled it an accident and the police did not investigate any further.

Although his demeanor and delivery hadn't changed—very matter-of-fact; I could see the intensity building in his eyes.

Then, a week ago, a 14 year old Lebanese boy, Perry Zoll, went missing. His parents contacted the police almost immediately and a search began. Two days ago, he was found wedged inside a roof vent for an AC unit on top of a local convenience store. Once again, the autopsy showed no drugs or alcohol and the coroner determined he died from a stress related heart attack. His parents said that he had never run away from home before and, as far as they knew, he had never even been to that convenience store before—even though it was less than three miles from his house. The coroner ruled it an accident, thinking he had wedged himself inside the unit, for some reason, and became stuck. The police are not likely to investigate it any further, Edmund thinks.

Despite my hot tea, I shivered at what must have been a horrible death.

Although I have never been much of a crime reporter, I have read my share of true crime stories and binge-watched tons of murder documentaries on Netflix; these deaths did not at all sound like the work of one person. A serial killer usually has a particular type of victim, a very specific manner of killing, they don't often have victims of different races, and above all else, not one of these deaths were even ruled as a homicide. I pointed all this out to Edmund. He just shrugged his shoulders and said, "I know." But he did it in such a cute way.

At this point, he said he had to get back to work, but asked if I would meet him again to discuss this more. I, of course, said yes. He replied he'll text me his availability. What is wrong with me? Why am I willing to meet with this guy? He's a little socially awkward, and just spouting another crazy conspiracy theory. But damn, there is something about him. He's kind of like a lost puppy and I just want to take him home and cuddle with him.

Saturday July 15, 2017

Dear Sam,
While slogging my way through a fluff piece about about artists in London doing something chivalrous for some charity, I got a text from Edmund asking to meet up again tomorrow. Even though I

really had no idea how I could help him with his theory, I agreed. Is it cute or pathetic that this one little text turned my whole day around?

It's been lonely since you've left. There's been a few app initiated rendezvous here and there, and a handful of random no hook-up dates but nothing long lasting. I've thrown myself into my work but I always have one eye on the door hoping against all reason that you'll walk back into my life. I know, it's been almost five years, but for some reason I can't let you go. You are the standard against I measure every guy I meet, and they all fall short, because they aren't you. My therapist is exasperated with me, I can't seem to move on. My pattern is to fall for a guy quickly and then just as quick realize he isn't you and then I do something overtly stupid to sabotage the relationship.

I've really have overloaded my work assignments. It's money and it keeps me from getting into too much trouble. The devil play hands are idle workers...or something like that. My friends, especially Sarah Brown, are getting concerned, there was some jocular talk amongst them of hiring me an escort...I hope they were joking. Well, I guess it depends on how hot the escort is...kidding.

Maybe this Edmund guy is just the thing to get me out of my dry spell.

Sunday July 16, 2017

Dear Sam,
I met Edmund at a tiny, tiny Indian restaurant that I didn't even know existed. It was surprisingly crowded, mostly with Indians-you know that means the food is good! He had gotten there early and had a table for us. Three or four of the staff were hanging about the table and he was chatting with them—in Hindi. Wow, that's impressive.

"I didn't know you spoke Hindi," I remarked as I sat down.

He blushed a little and said something about being a beginner.

The staff gushed that he was no beginner and joked that he spoke Hindi better than most of their own children.

After a bit of help from Edmund with the menu, we ordered. And while we waited for our food, I asked, "Why do you need my help with your theory? I'm not a crime expert."

"I understand that. I am not one either, but I am good at seeing patterns that aren't easy to see. The crux of my job is figuring out the pattern, finding the discrepancies and analyzing what they mean. With those skills, I have determined these crimes have the same pattern. What I'm not good at is convincing other people to listen to my theory, or to me, in general. You're the fourth person whose help I elicited and you're the first who has even agreed to give me a hearing."

Ouch! Ego deflated—I was fourth on his list.

"You think I can help you convince others of your theory?" I piped in, "How exactly? I'm a freelance writer, I don't have a regular column or anything."

"All I know is that you are good with words and people like you," he replied.

Ego re-inflated. People like me, he thinks people like me.

"That's very kind of you, but I'm not sure I can do much," I told him.

"Well, I disagree," he retorted brusquely. "You are the man I want."

My heart went pitter-patter for a beat even though I knew what he really meant. All during our conversation, Edmund was rearranging the condiments on the table, at first from shortest to tallest, then from lightest in color to darkest in color, and lastly in some order I didn't immediately recognize, until he remarked that the one closest to him was very spicy and I should take care if I should take that one. He did this reorganization without much conscious effort, it was as if he created order of out of chaos on an instinctual level.

At that point, our food arrived. I got the Chicken Vindaloo and he got something called Malai Kofta. I joked with him that sounded like an existential writer. He just looked at me. Swing and a miss! On a side note, one of the editors I work with said my writing is too lofty and inaccessible for most audiences. He wants me to use more commonly accepted colloquiums, so I am trying out sports metaphors.

Edmund and I made somewhat awkward small talk throughout the meal. As I tried to get to know him by asking the usual date-type questions, his replies were short and he rarely asked a question in return. Though the food was good, I was kind of ready to leave by the time we finished. My desire to date him was waning; as you know, so often I build up the other guy into something he really isn't, but then reality comes crashing in and destroys my straw man. Is that a sports metaphor? Is there a sport where people destroy straw dummies? Jousting, perhaps. He didn't really present his case to me well. (Or he didn't really well present his case? — no that sounds terrible).

As we were settling the bill, he looked me hard in the eyes and said, "Please, you're my only hope." Ok, Princess Leia, did you know you just made a Star Wars reference, you had to, right? But there was only sincerity in his eyes.

"Ok, let's meet again in a couple days and come with a strategy of how you want to get this out there and to whom." I relented.

He smiled—mostly at the fact I used "whom" correctly, I think.

Tuesday July 18, 2017

Dear Sam,
I happened to have the local news on this evening. The lead story, after the traffic and weather, was about an unusual death. A 24 year old Hispanic man was found dead in a park yesterday, and although his cause of death was undetermined at this point, and there was no sign of violence, the police were ruling his death suspicious.

Coincidence? Or did Edmund's serial killer strike again? Maybe I am just getting paranoid. People die all the time, and sometimes in very strange ways without the help of a murderer. Nevertheless, I'm texting Edmund in the morning. I did some serious rethinking about Edmund's datability, if he is really this smart to figure out that a serial killer is out murdering in Dayton, then maybe I should give him a second chance. Presuming of course, he is gay and he is open to dating and he's open to dating me.

Friday July 21, 2017

Dear Sam,
Edmund was unable to meet until today, the district attorney was going after a shady business owner who might have been laundering money and they needed Edmund's expertise. Fortunately, he was free by mid-afternoon and we met at the reflecting pools at Riverscape Park downtown. It's a great park with reflecting pools, ice skating rink and tons of plaques about the history of Dayton. I

almost suggested he come over to my place and I could make us dinner, but—too soon, too soon.

He immediately brought up the strange death of the young Hispanic man. He told me he had overheard two detectives talking about the case and they said the cause of death was a heart attack. In a 24 four year old? Edmund said that the police officers has commented that the coroner was stumped. There was no sign of heart disease and the man had been healthy otherwise. And I know I'm repeating myself, but there was no evidence of drugs or alcohol and he was less than three miles from his home.

When I asked what the man's name was, Edmund was slightly taken aback. Why would I want to know that, he asked.

He was a human, he has a name, he deserves to be known, I replied.

Edmund looked at me, cocked his head to one side (he is just so cute when he does that, like a little pup) as if he was trying to puzzle it all out.

"E. C. Culbertson," was the answer.

I remarked it didn't sound like a very Hispanic name to me. He countered that this man's mother had remarried when E. C. Was very young.

"Well, where do we go from here?" I asked.

Edmund looked at me and cocked his head (damn cute) and said, "We just have to tell people. Maybe print it in the paper. Like a paid advertisement maybe."

"You have two big problems with that. One, it costs money, a good amount of money perhaps, to pay for an ad like that. The second, I don't think the newspaper would print it. It would scare too many people."

"But they have to be warned," he cried.

He cares about people. He is not just a numbers nerd. He's real people. I smiled despite his desperation.

"Yes, but we have to get an authority like the police or some respected media figure to put forth the idea so people will take it seriously. If we wanted, we could throw it up on the internet, but I doubt many people would see it and even less believe it. Have you spoken to any one at the police department about this?"

With downcast eyes, he shook his head no.

Why, I asked.

"The police department treats me well and appreciates my talent. But some of the officers are not nice"

Ugh...bullying. They should know better.

"Is there any one officer, that you could talk to, we could talk to, that would at least hear us out?"

"Emily Sparks."

Monday July 24, 2017

Dear Sam,
Detective Sparks' office was a tiny, cluttered affair. A dilapidated desk and three well-used chairs occupied most of the square footage. But they could hardly be seen under the piles and piles of papers, files, evidence bags, fast food wrappers and a few things I couldn't easily or want to identify. There was not a spot in the room that wasn't buried under a pile of some sort.

She herself was well put together. An immaculate uniform, clean nails, hair neat, and just a touch of make-up. Snaps for Detective Sparks.

Less snaps when she pushed piles of papers off two of the chairs so we could sit down. I glanced at Edmund and could tell that he was not comfortable—this place was anathema to his neat and ordered world. He was as uncomfortable as a rookie batting clean-up (I'll confess that I just googled sports metaphors for some one who is feeling uncomfortable and this came up, I'm not sure exactly what it mean. But I get a point for trying). He began to straighten up the colossal mess, but Sparks ordered him to get to the point of his visit.

He began to tell his tale with much more confidence than before— maybe I buoyed him up. Snaps for me! She was absolutely attentive to him, never interrupting him, never checking her phone, not even taking notes. Sparks listened to every word that Edmund said and I just bobble-headed my agreements to his statements. After he had finished, she just looked at him for a long time. Not in hostility or disbelief, but trying to size him up. Finally, she spoke.

"Edmund, I know you are brilliant. You do wonders with the accounting stuff we give you, but there are no connections between these victims. They didn't live in the same neighborhoods, they didn't move in the same circles and they most certainly didn't die in the same manner. Nothing links them."

"I know that is how they appear on the surface, but these **are** murders and they are done by the same person." Edmund protested.

"Even if I wanted to believe that, I would need concrete proof before the upper brass would have these re-classified as homicides. I am not sure what I can do."

"Can't you issue a warning to the public about the possibility of serial killer so they could take precautions?" He pleaded.

"I can't. I don't have the authority to do that and again you have no proof. You could try and take this to the media, but I don't think they would give it much thought. You have nothing to go on other than your hunch, as good as your hunches usually are." She gently retorted.

"I'll find that proof. But I'll need you to do something for me" he stated.

She raised a supercilious eyebrow.

"I'll need the copies of the autopsy reports."

That request did not go over well.

"That's not possible. It would be an invasion of privacy and against a million police regulations."

"Please, I know if I could look at those reports, I can find the connection. I know I can do this." Edmund pleaded.

Oh, my little puppy looked sad, but I would brighten his day with my brilliant suggestion.

"Detective Sparks, what if you were to have those reports in your office and, say, leave them on a random pile while Edmund here was working with you, and you had to step out of the room to arrest a criminal or to go down to the shooting range or complain to someone about this drab decor?"

Problem solved.

This time the eyebrow was less supercilious.

"Come by tomorrow, but you have to promise that they stay in my office and that you do not copy them in any way, not even taking notes."

My puppy wagged his symbolic tail.

On our drive back to his car, I was jubilant.

"Let's celebrate. How about dinner, it's a little early, but I know this hibachi place, you'll love it."

Edmund looked at me expressionlessly.

"No thank you."

"But...but..." I stammered. How could he say no, after all the favors I did him? I did a quick exhale through the nose. Fine.

"Ok, maybe next time," I offered.

Ugh, now there was awkward failed date silence. The worst silence of all.

"Do you want me to come with you tomorrow to the police station?" I proffered.

"That won't be necessary."

Not necessary but very much desired.

"Ok, let me know how it goes tomorrow."

"I will and thank you for the ride," he said as he left my car and loneliness took his place. Ugh, when did my writing skills become so prosy.

Tuesday July 25, 2017

This has been a frustrating day. Not a peep from Edmund. I really thought we had a connection, but with hindsight, I might have been seeing more than what is really there. I am nearly climbing the walls of my apartment. I don't have a lot of work to do, it's just one of those rare occasion where I finished all the current work and sent it off, but the specs for the new pieces haven't arrived yet…such is the life of a modern day journalist.

I am tempted to jump onto Grindr or Hinge, but I made a promise to myself to reduce the number of randos; I hope I have the will power to keep it. Maybe, instead, I will have a chocolate chip cook and binge some Great British Bake-Off. Wish me strength.

Wednesday July 26, 2017

Dear Sam,
You didn't wish hard enough. But that might have turned out for the best. I went out on a date tonight, and I enjoyed it, but I, of course, found a way to ruin it. And the date was not hanging out with Edmund listening to his theories, it wasn't with Edmund at all. I caved to my baser desires last night and checked out my Hinge account (it had been a while since I had looked at it, I had to dust off the digital cobwebs). To my surprise, I had gotten a message from someone who wasn't asking for a dick pic or wanting to know if I was into some weird fetish. A couple weeks ago, I had swiped right on this guy. I was immediately attracted to his name—Gustav, and his pics were hot without being too-hot-to-be-real hot. He replied to my question about the weirdest gift he had ever received. He said that an elderly aunt had given him a rattan rooster with god awful fake feathers. She said she heard from her son that he liked cocks. I found that to be a pretty interesting answer, maybe there is hope for this one.

So, on a whim (not an act of desperation), I messaged him back and said that I didn't have any plans for this evening, if he wanted to meet for drinks. He replied that that he would prefer dinner and drinks; I acquiesced.   He suggested a local Mexican place which I happen to really like, so I acquiesced again.

I have a terrible tendency to arrive way early for dates as you'll remember from when we first started dating, an almost pathological fear of being late. I was there a good twenty minutes before our scheduled time and sat down in the restaurant's lobby. I was glad I wore a tight-but not too tight-fitting polo and my best skinny jeans. Even in the air conditioning, I was sweating the oh-my-god-is-this-guy-going-to-like-me pre-date sweat. And my palms were so sweaty; what is the evolutionary advantage of sweaty palms? And then for some reason my mind couldn't help but flash back to Edmund saying that people like me, I smiled. Good old Edmund, he really boosted my ego with that.

Right on time, Gustav walked through the door looking like his pics! Sam, you know how rare that is. And he was hot. Great hair, great smile, great sense of fashion—a modest T-shirt that framed his pecs nicely and shorts that were short enough to get my attention without being trashy. He had a good, solid handshake and spoke with such a sexy German accent.

We sat down and the conversation started right away—that's always a good sign. He is from Bremen, Germany and was sent over by his company-Mechrichttrabenlaftstag, or something like that, to scout out locations for a possible new branch of their firm. They make something shiny—I got lost in his eyes when he was giving me the details.

He asked the right questions and laughed at the right times, he even playfully bumped his leg against mine under the table a time or two. He moved at the right pace for me, not too fast, but fast enough to keep me interested. At the end of dinner, he suggested going for a drink at that quiet little gay bar downtown. Again, I agreed to his suggestion.

We drove separately and he had a table and a drink waiting for me by the time I arrived, he was scoring all sorts of bonus points. Our conversation continued unabated and we laughed and chatted and flirted. He was holding my hand across the table when he asked if we could go back to my place. (He was sharing a hotel suite with a coworker--a very nosy coworker).

I heard myself saying no. What? Why did I do that? He was hot and we were really getting along. I totally crushed him, he was so sure that I would say yes, I saw it in his eyes. To be honest, I was sure I would say yes until I didn't. He withdrew his hand and said he understood. I wish he would have explained it to me, cause I still don't.

My "no" killed the date; the conversation stopped; the laughter stopped and the flirting most definitely stopped. Ugh, why did I do this? I knew why, but I did understand the why. The why was Edmund but why Edmund? Why can't I accept that there is nothing going on between Edmund and I, and nothing will ever develop.

Gustav walked me to my car and to his credit he didn't ask me to reconsider his offer. He did ask if he could see me again. I lied when I said yes or at least I intended to lie. I didn't think I could see him any more. It felt like I was being unfaithful to Edmund.

I came home to a lonely apartment and I have a feeling I'm going to sleep terribly tonight.

Friday July 28, 2017

Dear Sam,
God damn it. Why do I do this to myself? I uber-fixate on a guy like Edmund who couldn't possibly be interested in me and then I pine over him and drive myself crazy waiting for him to reciprocate. All week, I've waited for him to contact me after his time viewing the autopsy reports. And I get nothing.

I could text Gustav and have a great time with him. But I don't. Why? He's smart, funny, intelligent and has such a sexy accent. Do you know the song by Vertical Horizon?

He's everything you want
He's everything you need…
He says all the right things
At exactly the right time
But he means nothing to you
And you don't know why.

Yep, that pretty much sums it up. But I can't let myself pursue Edmund like some love-starved teenager. I refuse to contact him. I have my self-esteem, I have my pride. I refuse to. Sigh, I might have self-esteem and pride, but I have no will power.

Saturday July 29, 2017

Dear Sam,
I texted him last night, Edmund not Gustav. And I stared at my phone for hours, why won't he text back? Maybe I should stop by his apartment just to check on him...oh I see it now, I've crossed the

line into stalkery. Enough of this, I am going to get some of my work done. I have a few pieces that need touching up so I can send them off and get paid. Alas, money, a most necessary evil.

Later, I did get a text from Gustav asking to meet up again. I said I was too busy with work and I'll get back to him.

Monday July 31, 2017

Dear Sam,
"We need to talk," the text read. Oh god, are we breaking up? That's what you say when you initiate the break-up conversation, right? Oh calm down, he doesn't know we are dating so he can't want to break up. Kidding-not kidding.

"Just tell me where and when" was my reply.

Tuesday August 1, 2017

Dear Sam,
"It doesn't make any sense," Edmund lamented. "I can sense that there is a pattern with these deaths, but I just can't see it. There has to be a connection."

I empathized with him, but he was becoming obsessed with these cases, but to be honest, my attention was split between him and the breakfast sandwich I gotten from my favorite coffee shop. The sandwich was winning. After the finishing, I took a hard look at Edmund. He looked terrible, hardly slept, probably didn't eat or even go outside in the sunshine—though I got the idea that he didn't normally spend much time out of doors. I didn't have the heart to tell him that there probably weren't any connections.

"This is really important to you," I offered as a condolence.

He just gave me that look. It is so hard to describe it. A look that blended incomprehension, confusion and touch of sadness in the corners of his eyes. Other than that, he didn't respond.

We sat in silence for a while. It was probably a comfortable silence for him, but for me, it was totes uncomfortable.

Just to banish the stillness, I asked, "Did you learn anything new about any of the deceased?"

He began to rattle off facts: "John Cabanis was a manager of a hardware store and had his appendix removed 13 years ago; Amelia Garrick, a lawyer, was injured in a car crash when she was 19 and won a significant settlement from the other driver for her injuries; Perry Zoll was a amateur chess player and diabetic, E.C. Culbertson did some hard drugs as a teen but had been clean for more than 5 years, he was in the process of adopting his girlfriend's daughter. They all had a pet of some kind. Do you think that's anything, having a pet?"

"Lots of people have pets," I replied. "Did they go to the same vet?"

"No, I checked," Edmund glumly retorted.

His cell phone rang—not a musical ring tone, but a boring pre-set ring. Doesn't he accessorize anything? He looked at the number cocked his head in his cute puppy way and answered it.

"Yes...really?...I can be there in 15 minutes. Can I bring Jonathan? Yes, he is the reporter."

Bring Jonathan? Who? Wait, that's me. He wants to take me somewhere. I was all rainbows and unicorns.

To me he said, "There's been another murder and they want me my opinion. Detective Sparks says you can come, but this has to be off the record, per Captain Burleson's edict."

"I agree." I chirped happily.

Edmund drove, which was a first for us. His driving didn't really alarm me, as much as it unnerved me. I had never driven with anyone who so ardently followed every traffic law, never speeding, never changing lanes without signaling, always smooth acceleration and braking, never even getting closer than three cars lengths to the person in front of us. Yeah, I know, unnerving.

To my surprise, we didn't go to the police station, but instead drove out on a rural road, passing fields of corn "that was as high as an elephant's eye." I know it's an old reference, but there aren't a lot of musicals about farming these days. And there are no sports metaphors about farming at all.

"Is this even in the city's jurisdiction?" I asked.

"Yes, there are a few rural parts like this that are still considered to be part of the municipality," Edmund stated flatly.

We stopped in front of a house with a ginormous barn and expansive fields. A host of police cars and rescue vehicles were parked on the gravel driveway. The uniformed police officer acting as a guard dog stopped us and took Edmund's name and checked his list. He then let us through.

Detective Sparks was waiting for us in front of the barn. She was wearing that facial expression that people reserve for when talking about the dead. Her uniform was again immaculate, but had on ugly mid-calf boots. I hope that was a practical rather than aesthetic choice.

"We have another death," she explained. "I thought this one might fit your pattern too. His name is Roscoe Purkapile..."

It took everything I had not to laugh...that can't really be his name!

"Age 61, white male, cause of death...um...a cow fell on him," Sparks said with as straight a face as she could muster.

Oh my god...there is nothing humorous in this, but really, a cow sitting on him? Really? I didn't laugh, but I did cough a little.

Edmund just looked at me with his look. "Why do you think this fits in with the others?" He asked the detective.

"The others were all freak accidents and this certainly qualifies as a freak accident. Come with me and I'll show you," she invited. "But don't touch anything." She added looking hard at me.

She led us behind the massive barn and into a corral. Several cows were standing and swishing their tails. None of them seemed particularly murderous. Ok, enough comedy.

On the ground was a human. There wasn't a lot of blood, but he was disfigured. The cow must have sat on his chest and crushed it.

"How could this have happened?" Edmund inquired.

"We aren't sure. We thought at first that maybe he had a stroke or heart attack and died then the cow tripped and fell on him, but the

EMTs think that unlikely. We are pretty sure he was still alive and moving when the cow landed on him." Sparks explained.

"Which cow did it," I asked.

Now I got that look from both Edmund and the detective.

"That one," Sparks pointed out a cow that pretty much look like all the other cows. "We found some blood on its backside."

One of the EMTs turned to the detective and said, "What if he fell into a diabetic coma? He is wearing an insulin pump."

"How sophisticated is it? Can you figure out his most recent blood sugar reading?" Asked Edmund.

"Yeah, sure. Let's see..." The EMT was pressing buttons on the device. "His last reading was at 12:44 pm and was 112. That's normal for a diabetic. The one before that was 123, again normal. And the one before that was 98. I guess it wasn't a diabetic coma."

"It was a good thought," Sparks condoled.

Edmund had wandered off a little down the field, his fingers were moving as if he was counting. His lips moved, but no sound was coming out. His face was scrunched up in serious thought.

"Maybe this is a connection, Purkapile and Zoll both had diabetes," he worked out his thought aloud.

"Yeah, but did any of the others?" Sparks asked.

"No, but in the autopsy report it stated that Culbertson had a vitamin D deficiency," Edmund went on.

The detective and I both just looked at him. Where was he going with this?

"Jonathan, look up treatment for vitamin D deficiency," Edmund asked, really ordered.

Regardless, anything for you.

"Wikipedia says that it can be treated by pills or injection," I read.

The detective's eyes lit up. Sparks hurriedly dialed her phone and was talking with the coroner in just a few minutes. She asked him about the other two victims.

"Cabanis occasionally took injections for his migraines and Garrick had deep vein thrombosis which is also treated by injections. That's something all have in common, but I'm not sure it's anything more than coincidence." She stated.

"What are you getting at?" I asked Edmund.

"What if they were injected with something that paralyzed them or made them compliant? The killer could then easily arrange these "freak accidents." The coroner wouldn't note the injection marks as anything out of the ordinary because they would be expected since each victim took injections, it could be easily overlooked." Edmund explained.

"That really seems unlikely," Sparks put in. "The killer would have to know an awful lot about his victims before he attacked them."

"As unlikely as a cow sitting on a man and killing him?" I defended my little pup. "But I thought you said that there were no drugs or alcohol found in any of the victims?"

"It is a common mistake to think that the labs test for every possible drug," Sparks explained, "they test for the common ones like cocaine, meth, ruffies or painkillers. It would take forever to test for the millions of drugs out there and it would be a huge waste of money. If we suspect a particular drug, we can test for that drug."

"What drug should we test for?" I asked.

"Curare," replied Edmund without missing a beat.

My puppy is so smart, but what?

"Curare? That drug that villains use in movies to paralyze people?" Sparks inquired.

"Yes, it would render the victims unconscious but not stiff so the murderer can still manipulate their bodies. It would be the perfect drug for him," Edmund replied.

"Where in the world would someone get curare? Is it still used in medicine today? Can you get a prescription for it at the pharmacy?" I snarkily asked. I pulled out my iPhone to start doing some research.

"I doubt it," Sparks stated. "But maybe there are modern drugs that would have a similar effect."

"There are. Two of the most common are Pancuronium and Rocuronium Bromide," I offered, reading off my iPhone.

"That means we are looking for someone who has access to drugs like that," Sparks said. "Your friendly, neighborhood dealer won't have those. I'll get the coroner to test for those on the victims."

I could see it on Edmund's face that he was elated to be proven right. I wanted to share in his accomplishment. So, I took a few steps towards Edmund to congratulate him and suddenly I'm on my back laying in what is affectionately known as "cow patties." Ugh, my best pair of skinny jeans are now covered in shit.

Detective Sparks and the EMTs roared into laughter and then moved to help me up. Edmund just stood there with a blank expression on his face and did nothing. Some boyfriend, huh? They helped me to my feet. I was covered in effervescent cow excrement and I stood there not sure what I should do. I wished I would have heeded Douglas Adams' advice and brought a towel.

Trying not to think about what my pants were covered in, I made my way back towards the car with Edmund, squishing all the way. He said he had an old blanket in his trunk I could use to wipe off. As we passed the house, I saw Mrs. Purkapile on the front porch, quietly crying with a police officer keeping her company. She happened to look up and see us.

"My word! What happened to you?" She asked.

"I slipped in the cow fence area," I sheepishly replied. Damn, you would never know I write for a living.

"You come on in and I'll take care of you," she responded.

Before I could say no, Edmund steered me towards the house. As I approached the front door, I slipped off my shoes and gingerly stepped inside. Mrs. Purkapile beckoned me further in.

"You can use the bathroom here to get out of your clothes. I have some of my son's old things still here, they will probably fit you. You can throw your things in the tub and give them a good rinse," she was off before I could protest. I had quite the time extricating myself from my shirt, it stuck to me like glue, foul smelling, squishy glue. The pants came off easily enough (I have had a lot of practice at this!), and I put them in the mint green 1970s bathtub and started running the water to rinse them out as best I could. At that moment, standing in my Andrew Christian briefs, which hide little, Edmund opened the door with some clothes for me. He looked down, then at my face, then looked down at me again. He sort of froze with one of his incomprehensible expressions. But for the first time since I met him, my gaydar pinged off him. Maybe, just maybe, my instincts are right.

He handed me the clothes and left without a word.

After dressing in some white painter pants and a red plaid shirt (oh, you know I made it work), I tidied up a bit, I placed my sodden clothes in a plastic grocery bag that Mrs. Purkapile had sent in with Edmund. I exited the bathroom and cast about to see where she had gone; I was in her debt and wished to thank her. I walked out on the front porch and found her there sitting placidly; she invited me to sit down.

"I am so sorry about your husband," I said.

"That is sweet of you, I am still in shock, I'm sure it will hit me when you all leave," she responded.

I asked if she had someone to come and stay with her; and she told me that her son, who lives in Chicago, is on his way and would be there in a couple of hours. How long have you been a police officer was her next question to me. I found it a little awkward trying to explain my presence there. I told her that I was with my friend who was lending his expertise to the police. I felt really out of place here, especially after my little slip in the mud. My hair was still matted down with gunk. I was trying to free some trapped water (oh god, I hope it was water) from my right ear when she dropped quite the surprise.

"What happened to the man in the black van?"

I'm sorry, what? What man in what black van? There was a man in a black van?

"Earlier today, I saw a black van pull into the driveway. A man got out and my husband went over to speak with him. We are selling some of the goats and people do occasionally stop by inquiring about them." She stated. "I thought it was just someone like that."

"And you didn't see him leave?" I asked.

"No, I was doing some cleaning," she went on to say,"After a good while, I went to see what the visitor wanted and that's when I found Roscoe."

Holy crap! This is it! First, super-sad that she found her husband dead that way, but she might have actually seen the killer! I jumped up and ran halfway back to the barn before turning around and gushing out my thank to Mrs. Purkapile again for her hospitality and again expressed my condolences and told her that she needed to tell the police about the man.

I ran back to the corral, suppressing my naturals instinct to scream and flail my arms about. I stood at the gate beckoning over Edmund and Detective Sparks.

"I have something to tell you," I hissed through my teeth as if I were finally revealing who shot Kennedy. "Mrs. Purkapile saw the killer!"

Both the Detective and my imagined boyfriend looked at me and Sparks said, "We know. She told us that earlier. I do question the witnesses, kinda my job."

Snarky, everyone thinks they can do snarky. I was the original snark. But I felt like an ass anyways. Running around thinking I solved the case. By any and all accounts, this was not my best day.

Friday August 4, 2017

Dear Sam,
Despite my ardent zeal that the details about Purkapile's mysterious visitor would blow the case wide open, there wasn't much movement on the case. After the farm events, Edmund drove me home and we did talk, but only about the murders. He seems oblivious to everything else. He is so focused on this serial killer, I'm sure it's not healthy for him.

Since then, I haven't heard from him once and I have not texted him, I am so proud of myself—two whole days without me contacting him. Thinking about him obsessively, yes; but calling him, no. I did get a text from Gustav asking if I had any plans for Saturday.

This weekend, one of my friends is having a BBQ (most of the them are vegans, so that means soy hot dogs and sawdust burgers—ick). I thought maybe I would invite someone to go with me. But whom? Gustav would be great company and make all my frenemies at the party supes jealous. He's a great conversationalist and totes gregarious. But maybe I should invite Edmund. It would be nice to get to know him better as a person before I declare him my boyfriend and start planning our wedding. I don't know what to do. Gustav wants to spend time with me, getting to know me, Edmund doesn't want to do anything other than discuss the murders. Gustav is funny and optimistic and Edmund isn't. Edmund doesn't have any checks in the good boyfriend material column and Gustav has them all. If this is so, why am I leaning towards inviting Edmund?

And even if I do invite Edmund, I don't think he'll accept. Ok, so that maybe will solve my problem. I'll invite Edmund, he'll say no and then I'll invite Gustav.

Saturday August 5, 2017

Dear Sam,
I was wrong again. I invited Edmund and he, shockingly, accepted. Well, shut my mouth! He accepted. Then he told me he was only going to get his parents off his back—they keep pushing him to do more social things. Well, I am glad that I could help Edmund escape the nagging of his parents—just a tad of sarcasm, if you couldn't tell.

I picked him up around six. As he got into my car I noticed he was dressed in a dull gray, short sleeve dress shirt and khakis. I, on the other hand, was sporting a tank-top hoodie, robin's egg blue, printed board shorts and flip-flops—fashionista that I am.

"Edmund, are you sure you'll be comfortable in those clothes, we will be outside," I prompted.

"I'm perfectly comfortable," he replied.

"I'm not. Don't you have something more...festive?" I offered.

"Like a Christmas sweater?" He quipped.

Yes! Not to the Christmas sweater, but yes to Edmund making a joke! I am so proud of him. I smiled more broadly than the joke called for; I wanted to encourage him.

"I like your thinking, but maybe something more beachy," I said.

"I don't have anything beachy, there isn't a beach for 606 miles." He retorted.

"What about Lake Erie, that's a lot closer than 606 miles." Right back at ya, puppy.

"Are we going to Lake Erie?"

Damn that supercilious eyebrow.

"No...but, there is a swimming pool." I stated.

"Oh, you didn't tell me that. I'll be right back." With that, he hopped out of my car and went back into his apartment.

I was feeling really proud of myself, helping him to be a more social member of society and a better dresser. We all know that what the world needs now is better dressers.

That feeling of pride lasted only until I saw him emerge from his apartment. Oh god, what have I done? He was now wearing a black, long sleeved wet suit top, baggy awful red swim trunks and (I'm not kidding) an umbrella hat. Oh, I have a lot, a lot of work to do.

"You cannot wear that hat," I demanded.

"I don't want to get sunburned," he explained.

"There are other ways to not get sunburned, I have sunscreen," I retorted.

With that settled, we drove to the party. Thankfully, I convinced him to leave the umbrella hat in the car and we joined the festivities. I could tell that this was way outside his comfort zone. He was quiet and kept close to me during the first hour or so of the party. Which, I'll admit, was nice, it was almost like having a boyfriend. But he didn't really engage in much conversation. And we decided ahead of time not to bring up the serial killer stuff, it would not be appropriate for this venue. So, without that topic, he seemed like he really didn't have much to say.

After a while, I found myself apart from him. He was exploring the landscaping around the backyard and I was chatting with my friend Sarah who was hosting.

"He seems nice," she stated. "Are you two...?"

"No, no, he's just a friend," I replied.

"For now?" She queried. She knows me too well.

I explained that we were working on a project together and I had grown fond of him. She thought that he seemed a little odd and definitely an introvert, and not at all my type.

I know. Gustav is my type. She would have loved, **loved** Gustav.

The next thing I know, Edmund was walking over to us with a three foot tall plant in his hand that he had evidently pulled out of Sarah's yard. My first reaction was to apologize to her.

"This is Phytolacca Americana," Edmund stated with his usual brusqueness, "It's potently poisonous. You need to remove it from your landscape."

It's what what with what?

"Phytolacca Americana, also called Pokeweed, Poke Sallet or Dragonberries. It is toxic to mammals in its raw form. Though I guess you could be cultivating it to use in cooking. Is that the case?"

"No," Sarah murmured. Clearly stunned by Edmund's abrasiveness and obscure knowledge.

"Edmund, are you saying that if someone eats that, they could die," I tried to run interference here (snaps for me for using another sports analogy).

"Not only humans, but you have dogs, right? If they ate any part of this plant, they could become seriously ill," Edmund added.

At that moment, Lyman King interrupted us. I really don't like Lyman King.

"Oh, who is the brainiac with no fashion sense?" Lyman hissed. I really don't like Lyman King.

"Lyman, this is Edmund Pollard. Edmund this is Liar-man King. He is a journalist, of sorts. How's that article on the werewolf boy for the Enquirer coming?" I couldn't help myself.

"So, very droll. With your way with words, I'm surprised you haven't won a Pulitzer yet," Lyman spat out. "Jonny, is this your new beau?"

I was worried about Edmund's reaction, but true to form, he didn't react at all.

"No, just a friend. I see you are flying solo these days," Point for Jonathan!

"Who has time for a boyfriend with all the work I'm getting. I got a piece published in Columbus Monthly a few weeks ago." Lyman boasted.

"Oh, congrats! What was the piece about?" I inquired knowingly.

"The current fashion trends in goth bridal dresses," He said proudly with just a hint of doubt in his eye.

"Oh, I'm sure the Pulitzer committee has already taken note of that."

Lyman's only response was a sneer and then to wander away.

Point and match for Jonathan. I went back to the conversation with Sarah and Edmund. My puppy went on about different poisonous plants that people commonly use in their landscaping. Sarah wasn't interested at all in the topic, but I could tell she was as fascinated by Edmund as a person as I was. A few, long minutes later, Edmund excused himself to get another Diet Coke and Sarah bombarded me with questions.

"Where did you meet this guy?" She asked.

I explained that I had met him briefly years ago, but reconnected with him last month. I told her about how I'm helping him with an investigation, but didn't tell her about what. I played the angle that it was a possible story idea for me and I was hoping that this piece would get me more notoriety. She wanted to know "what his deal was," meaning was he gay or what, and I honestly replied that I didn't know.

"Jonathan, I know you. You are definitely into him. Are you chasing another man you can't get?" She bluntly asked.

Maybe. "Maybe."

She, as a good friend would, admonished me that this was not healthy and I should find myself someone else. I decided to tell her about Gustav. I could have predicted her reaction, she nearly screamed at me that that's who I should be dating. Sarah demanded I bring him to movie night at her place next Saturday. She joked (well, maybe semi-joked) that if I didn't bring Gustav that she would end our friendship then and there. Eek. I guess I'm bringing Gustav.

The rest of the party passed without incident. Edmund came out of his shell a little and chatted with a good number of the guests on his own. I would go around and check on him from time to time, but he said he was doing fine and I think maybe he enjoyed himself. No, I know he definitely did. He told me so. And then he thanked me for taking him. Wow, maybe my puppy is growing up.

I decided to brave the topic of sexuality. (Not directly, more of an end run (super snaps for me—another sports analogy)).

"Did anyone there catch your eye?" I asked vaguely.

He just did his little cute cock of the head, not sure what I was asking.

"Did anyone there seem like someone you would want to date or get to know better, ya know," I stumbled over my words, for some reason feeling awkward.

'I don't date," was his flat reply. I couldn't tell from the tone of his voice what exactly he meant. He doesn't date because he doesn't want to, he doesn't date because there aren't many people he is interested in, he doesn't date because he took a vow of celibacy?

And you, my puppy, don't know it, but you do date—you are dating me!

Wednesday August 9, 2017

Dear Sam,

I just returned from a date with Gustav. (My, but my dance card is filling up). I took a good hard look at myself at the bequest of my therapist. He agreed with Sarah and strongly encouraged me to give Gustav another go. He quite literally kicked my butt and told me to spend more time with my German stud. I might have grounds for a grievance, my therapist refused to talk to me until I spent more time with Gustav. It was a good therapeutic technique.

The evening with Gustav was wonderful, fun, and flirty. It almost made me forget about Edmond. I reasoned since Sarah was forcing me to bring Gustav on Saturday, I thought I should spend a little more time with him. He was thrilled when I texted him, making me feel even guiltier. I really should have spent more time with him or maybe no time with him and more time with Edmund. I'm like a kid staring at the list of possibilities in an ice cream shop; I really don't know what I want. Despite my indecision, I went out with Gustav.

Anyways, I asked him if he'd like to go to a movie. He poo-pooed that idea. He said that movies make for terrible dates since you can't really talk and get to know the other person. Miniature golf was his alternative. Really? What am I, twelve years old? Not wanting to be so snarky, I expressed my reluctance in a more respectful way. But he laid out a convincing case: One, it gave us an activity to focus on instead of staring at each other across a table. Two, it provided abundant opportunities for new topics of discussion. Three, it revealed how competitive we each can be. Four, it showed how we deal with success and failure. And five, it was great people watching territory.

It was hard to argue against that.

On the drive home, we discussed the how the game went. He said he won, but I definitely had the higher score. But the competition wasn't really what kept me interested. It was our flirtatious interactions. There were even a few times that he showed me how to better hold my stick, it's called a golf stick, right? He would stand behind me and wrap his arms around me and position my hands on the club (yikes, this is fraught with sexual symbolism). It felt so good to be flirted with and desired and chased and touched. I am usually the one doing the chasing, often with little success. But tonight, Gustav caught his prey. Wait, wait one PG-13 moment, let me clarify. We did make out like horny teenagers, but nothing more. He is so incredibly patient. When I said stop, he stopped. I could really fall for this guy. He is on the fast track to boyfriend status.

Just when I am setting my heart on Gustav, I get a text from Edmund: "We need to meet up and talk." Facebook knew what it was doing when it came up with the "It's complicated" tag.

Thursday August 10, 2017

Dear Sam,
I met up with Edmund at this little hole-in-the-wall breakfast place, that again, I never knew existed. He must eat out a lot to find all these places. The food was fantastic, I highly recommend the Bourbon French Toast—out of this world! I'm going to have to stop meeting Edmund at restaurants or I'll have to buy (more) Lululemon stretchy pants.

"The police have found out a lot more since Mr. Purkapile's death," Edmund said. "They are treating all these deaths as homicides. The lab confirmed the presence of Rocuronium Bromide in all the victims and the cow, that's how the murderer got the cow to sit on him."

"That's great that the police are believing you now," I told him in most most encouraging voice.

"Yes, but the down side is that now that they are homicides, the police are restricting how much information they are giving out—even to me," he lamented. "But I'm not done with this. They can't see the patterns like I can. They still have no idea how he is choosing his victims, I can help with that."

"I'm sure the Police will manage," I said as delicately as I could.

"They would never have even known these were murders but for me. I don't know why they won't let me help." Edmund complained.

Wanting to change the subject, I asked, "Did anything come of the man and the black van that Mrs. Purkapile saw?"

"Not much. The police confirmed that there was a black van in that area around the time of the murder, two neighbors and a mailman all say they saw it. But that's about it. No one could identify the driver or license plate number," He reported. "I'm sure the police are in over their heads on this."

My little puppy won't let go of his bone!

We discussed the case some more with no new bits of information revealed. We had finished up our breakfast and were just sipping our tea. That is one thing we have in common, we both hate coffee and adore tea. I smiled at that thought, we do have things in common.

Edmund finished his tea and stated that he had to be at the police station to work on an unrelated case in 20 minutes. As we were standing up to leave and go our separate ways, once again, my puppy surprised me.

"What did you do last night?" he asked out of nowhere.

I'm sorry, what? This is the very first time Edmund had asked a question about my personal life. Um...last night, I, um, used miniature golf to flirt with an amazing man and played some tongue war with him after, why do you ask?

"Oh, I had a date," I simply replied. Oh my god, I felt so guilty. I cheated on him, even though I am not really dating Edmund. Should I have lied to spare his feelings?

I closely watched his reaction. Again, his unfathomable expression with a slight hint of confusion was all he revealed. Did I expect him to be jealous?

Not knowing what to say next, I asked him about his evening. He stayed home and did some reading. He had a book on Egyptology, another on new techniques in forensic accounting and some things on serial killers that he found online. He gave me a brief (brief being a relative term when it comes to Edmund) summary of each of his readings. He was a little more conversational than he usually was. Maybe I'm having a positive impact on him.

I'm such a giving person—two gold stars and a reading rainbow for me!

Saturday August 12, 2017

Dear Sam,
Today was a busy day. It started with a text from Edmund asking to meet for lunch today to discuss his favorite topic and that was quickly followed by a text from Gustav containing some rather

naughty vegetables. Do I have two men vying for my attention? Oh yes, yes I do!

I agreed to Edmund's lunch and then retexted some naughty vegetables of my own to Gustav. I had to finish up some writing before I met with my puppy and then I thought, for Gustav, I should do some crunches to firm up my six pack...um, four pack...two pack...a one pack and nicely placed mole is really all I have. But I did a couple anyway.

Edmund recommended a Lebanese restaurant that was way on the other side of town. I knew it was going to be good, but damn it was a drive. As per our routine, he was already there and had a table for us. I slid into the seat across from and asked what was good on the menu.

"I don't know, I've never been here before," he said with an odd tone in his voice.

I asked him what's up, since this didn't seem like him.

"This restaurant is owned by Perry Zoll's parents," he whispered.

"The 14 year old who was murdered? What? Are you crazy? This is wrong. Really, really wrong. You haven't said anything to them about their son, have you?" I blurted out in a hushed whisper.

"No, but I thought we could ask them about his death," he put forth.

"No, no, no, in no way, this is completely inappropriate." I insisted that he say nothing.

It was just like disciplining a little dog, he sat there with sad puppy eyes and was very quiet.

Our meal was excellent but the mood sullen. Like the rest of us, Edmund didn't like being told no. I talked with him about how we can still have a part in the investigation, but it just won't be as active. It was clear that he was not to be dissuaded, though he didn't say anything against what I said. Edmund was certainly not earning any boyfriend points with this lunch.

After this dreary (but delicious) lunch, I was eagerly looking forward to my time with Gustav. I was hoping tonight not to tell him no. I had a bit more writing and researching to do, before I would spend laborious hours getting ready for this date. I won't go into all the details, just the usual gay man pre-date checklist: a little gelling, a little shaving, a little 'scaping, some assiduous teeth brushing and a dab of Musc Ravageur. I decided to forgo the skinny jeans even though they had been thoroughly washed several times (maybe because they still carried the aroma of la bovine, or perhaps it was just the memory of it!). Shorts were a better decision anyway, sitting close together on a couch to watch a movie could become a sweaty mess if I overheated, and a little bare calf would allow for some leg on leg action with Gustav! I decided to go with my gray shorts with my dark blue sleeveless hoodie (I have a thing for hoodies) and sandals. Tonight was all about comfort and relaxation. I was so looking forward to spending this time with Gustav and introducing him to my friends.

Gustav picked me up around 6:45. He had to work late unexpectedly but still had time to stop home and get himself looking fabulous. I got a hello kiss, very nice. And he noticed both my cologne and my shorts. "You look good in shorts," he said. I blushed a bit—which, to be honest, wasn't totally sincere—oh girl, I know I look good in shorts!

We chatted on the short drive to Sarah's. He talked about work, some negotiations with the city about zoning stuff and lawyers and paper work. It didn't really matter what he talked about, I could listen to his accent all night.

At the last minute, he took a wrong turn, but when I gently corrected him, he said that we had a stop to make first. We pulled into the parking lot of a little quaint bakery which (once again) I had no knowledge of—I have to get out more, this is my home town after all!

I pointed out that the sign said they were closed, he replied, "Not for us." He hopped out and rapped on the glass entrance. An elderly woman opened the door and smiled broadly at Gustav.

"Mama," he cried as he hugged her.

Wait! I'm meeting his mother? I am not prepared for that, let alone dressed for that. I didn't even know she was in America. This is going to cost him many boyfriend points, *many*. Oh, crap, I'm not ready for this.

"Mama, this is Jonathan Swift Somers. Jonathan, this is Mama Wertman. When I first came to the city, I found this bakery and

Mama adopted me as a long lost son. She is from the same part of Germany I am and some of her family knows some of mine. She helped me so much in those first few weeks." Sigh of relief—not his real mom.

"He is even more handsome than you described, Gustav," she cooed to him.

Me handsome? I am really more striking than handsome. I thanked her and told her how nice it was to meet her. She then handed Gustav a large brown paper bag, filled with something wafted a smell of sheer deliciousnesses.

"It's one of her world famous giant soft pretzels. People come over from Germany just to get one," Gustav explained.

"He exaggerates," was her humble response.

"I hope I didn't keep you too long," Gustav stated.

"No, no, I am happy to do this for you and your (she paused here for emphasis) boyfriend," she teased giddily.

Gustav blushed a bit. I could tell he was worried about my reaction to that. I was fine with it. I think he has earned enough boyfriend points for me to be called his boyfriend.

We both thanked Mama Wertman and sped off to Sarah's, arriving fashionably late. Our host greeted us warmly and didn't even chide us for being tardy. She was very impressed with the ginormous pretzel (as well as being very impressed with Gustav) and set the salty thing of goodness out with the other snacks. I, meanwhile, introduced everyone to Gustav. To my chagrin, Lyman was there. I really don't like Lyman King.

"Oh, I see you traded-in the nerd for some eye candy," Lyman sneered. If it helps, picture him with an evil handle-bar mustache—I always do.

"Jealous much?" I snarkily replied. Gustav and I took a seat on the end of the couch. I scrunched a little closer to him than I had to, but when you got it, flaunt it.

"I hope you all are ready to be creeped out!" Sarah announced. "Tonight's main feature is <u>The Voices</u>. Not the terrible TV show. This is a horror flick starring Ryan Reynolds."

Speaking of eye candy, Ryan Reynolds very tasty.

"It's a little dark and twisted. The movie tells the tale of how a seemingly ordinary guy can become a serial killer." She added eerily.

"Jonathan can tell us all about serial killers, right?" Lyman hissed out.

I can do what to who? What was he getting at? How did he know? What does he know?

But our attention was diverted by a comment from one of the other guests who said she had read a good review of this. Sarah dimmed the light, started the film and I snuggled up a little closer to Gustav; he put his arm around me. I could get used to this.

The opening scene of the movie is Ryan Reynolds in pink overhauls. Not a bad beginning.

Then...from my pocket, the theme from <u>Big Bang Theory</u> started playing. It was the ringtone I picked for Edmund; he would be right at home on that show.

Moans and groans ran up and down the couch, I should have silenced my cell before the movie began. But Edmund has never called me before, always texted. Ugh, I had to answer this. I reluctantly extricated myself from the comfort of Gustav and stepped into the kitchen.

"Edmund, this isn't a good time," I barked.

"There's been another killing and the police have invited me, well, us, to the scene. You should be here to help," He explained.

Ugh. No. Ugh. No. Ugh. Yes.

How was I going to explain this to Gustav? He has been so wonderful, maybe, he'll possibly understand. Maybe he'll give up on me like he probably should have a while ago.

I told Edmund I would meet him at the location of the murder, but it might be a while. "Hurry," was his only response. No "thank you,' no "great I will really need your support." Just "Hurry." Edmund you have terrible timing.

I took a deep breath and poked my head back into the living room and said, "Gustav, can I talk to you for a mini-minute?" Gustav came in concerned and asked if everything was all right. God, how do I begin? I said yes, everything was all right but I had a friend in need and I had to go help him.

Once again, I saw that crushed look in his eye. "Oh," he said.

He deserved the whole story. I told him about Edmund and how we reconnected early this summer and how we have been working together to help the police track down a serial killer and Edmund was the one who figured it all out and that Edmund was a little socially awkward and needed my help in dealing with the police and he didn't have anyone else to turn to and there's been another killing tonight and the police have invited Edmund to the scene for his input and Edmund called me for my help and support and even though you and I are on date, I told him I would meet him there and one more thing, I might have a little crush on him.

Gustav titled his head in that confused manner like Edmund does — so damn cute.

I waited for him to say something. It was clear he was working this through, deciding whether he believed me or not.

"I understand if you just want to walk away from me and my mess," I murmured.

"Don't be ridiculous, the right thing to do would be to help your friend," he replied after a moment. Who *is* this guy? Why is he this nice? Great, I'm back to feeling guilty and undeserving. I made our apologies to our host and explained that a friend has taken ill and we had to go. She was suspicious, but decided not to press the issue, for now. She did give me you-owe-me-an-explanation look. I mouthed the words "I will" to her.

On my way out, I went into the kitchen and nabbed a mighty chunk of that awesome giant pretzel for the road. We got back into his car and I just stared at the lump of pretzel in my hands. Gustav was uncharacteristically quiet as we drove across town.

"You haven't said much," I offered weakly.

"I haven't. This is a lot to take in. A serial killer, the police, a secret boyfriend," he stated.

"Whoa, whoa, Edmund is not my boyfriend. He is a guy I am helping who I have some minor feelings for," I explained.

"How minor?" Asked Gustav.

"I don't know. It's all confusing. Gustav, I really, really like you and have so enjoyed our time at Mexican place and mini-golf and meeting Mama Wertman. And I want to spend way more time with you and could see our relationship developing into something significant. It has been a long time since I have connected with someone like I am connecting with you. But Edmund is like a lost puppy, he needs me and I guess I am attracted to helping him." I gibber-jabbered on. "I don't even know if he is gay."

"You are chasing this guy and you don't know if he is gay? Has he shown any sign of being interested in you?" Damn, Gustav asks hard questions.

"No, maybe, not really, maybe I am seeing more than is there," I finally admitted. Ashamed at how foolish I must have seemed.

There was a long pause. And I might have shed a tear at my childish infatuation. Then I felt a warm, strong hand hold mine.

"Then I only have one more question for you, are you willing to get some dinner with me later after your errand is finished? — I'm starving," he said with a smile. I offered him the some of the pretzel chunk and said yes.

A few minutes later, we arrived at the address that Edmund had texted me. It was a beautiful, old Tudor style home in the swankiest part of town. The police waved us through once I had given them my name. Edmund and Detective Sparks were waiting for us (well, really me) at the large fountain in front of the main doors. I felt decidedly awkward bringing my new boyfriend (not officially yet) to meet my old boyfriend (not ever really) at a murder scene. Are other people's lives this complicated or am I just lucky?

I parked the car along the circuitous drive way. We got out and walked toward the front doors. Both Edmund and the Detective raised eyebrows at Gustav. I hurriedly made introductions, fumbling through what appellation to apply to my new...boyfriend, friend, my ride, my body guard, Mama Wertman's adopted son...see my problem? I ended up introducing him as Gustav.

Sparks was apparently out on the town tonight as well. She was dressed in a simple but elegant LBD: "One is never over-dressed or underdressed with a Little Black Dress." I told you, Project Runway junkie.

Edmund rushed, well, not rushed, moved quicker than he normally moved, to my side and began to hurriedly talk completely ignoring Gustav. He might as well been a lamppost. Before he got out more than a few words, the Detective stopped him.

"You can't discuss this case in front of..." she said motioning towards Gustav, "No offense, but you haven't been cleared for this."

Being Gustav, he accepted this with grace and went back to his car. A spark of anger flared through me at this, how dare she banish Gustav, but I knew she was right. And moreover, there was no reason to give Gustav nightmares like the ones I've been having.

As Sparks guided us through the palatial house to an upstairs bathroom, she explained that she just arrived herself. The detective had foolishly thought that she could spend an evening out with her fiancé, but this little detour had changed her plans. I know the feeling. Outside the room stood another detective, one I didn't know, who was flipping through his little Blue Clues notebook. He was of medium height and weight, middle aged-ish, very nondescript, other than he was wearing the tired cliche of a trench coat. Why is fashion so hard for people?

"This is Detective Walter Simmons, he was first on the scene and thought this fit our killer's pattern," she explained.

"Prepare yourself, you probably haven't seen anything like this before —it's not pretty. She was pretty, but now," He prattled awkwardly.

Ew.

Opening the door with a little too much dramatic flair, the scene was revealed to us. In the tub (more like small swimming pool by the size of it) was the body of a young woman, floating face down. She had a bluish tint to her skin. Around the floor next to the bathtub was drug paraphernalia, syringes, pill bottles and such. Something was odd about this scene, I think it was that there really wasn't anything odd about this scene. It looked like a woman ODed and drowned in a bathtub. But being a novice in all this, I'm sure that I missed important clues. I looked to Edmund to explain this scene; I was quite sure he had already figured it out.

I was wrong again.

"This is not the work of our serial killer," Edmund stated bluntly.

"Wait, just wait a damn minute, she was an IV drug user, so again, he covered his tracks by picking a victim expected to have needle marks. And, what if I told you, that the victim doesn't live here," Simmons said defensively.

"Where does she live? Have you identified her?" Edmund asked in a bored voice.

"Yes, her name is Jennie M'Grew and she lives a few streets over. She does have priors for drug possession and solicitation. The killer probably knew that the owners of the house were out of town and snuck in here with the vic. And he staged it to look like an overdose. Clever of him, I think," Simmons stated.

"An unlikely scenario, and here's why: 1. Never before has he killed a victim inside a building. All the others were outdoors. 2. There is nothing bizarre about this death like being struck by a fallen power line or being sat on by a cow. 3. This doesn't seem like his type of victim. With her drug addiction, she would already be too easily manipulated. Our killer likes a challenge. He picks victims that are not on the fringes of society, but from the very core, a farmer, a child, a business woman. You did not think this through very clearly." Edmund said in his rather brusque manner that Detective Simmons did not seem to appreciate.

"What the hell do you know? Are you a detective—no. Are you a criminal profiler—no. You're just an accountant with delusions of grandeur," he bellowed vociferously. The noise was such that a uniformed officer came running up the stairs to see what the ruckus was about. He stopped short bewildered.

Simmons looked at Sparks who said nothing but pursed her lips in a disapproving way. Which, apparently, the other detective also didn't like and so he pushed by the officer at the top of the stairs and huffed and puffed down the stairs.

"God damn it, Walter, you called me away from a dinner at CoCo's for this? Do you know what that costs? And now I get to microwave a great meal into a crappy one." Sparks hollered after him.

"Did you know that you can use the oven instead..." Edmund unwisely began to advise her on reheating food.

"Shut up, Edmund," She barked back at him.

Oh, my puppy got a verbal slap down. He's sad.

After a moment she apologized. "You have no idea how much I was looking forward to this night with my boyfriend." I do have some idea. "This is the first weekend in months that I got to do something coming close to normal with my fiancé. And what happens? Simmons jumps the gun. He is relatively new to the department and has been bucking for a promotion. He obviously thought that if he helped solve this serial killer thing, he would get it." She sighed deeply. A few moments of silence passed before she asked, "So, what were you two up to this evening before Simmons ruined it?"

"I was home," Edmund said succinctly.

"I was not at home," I said with some hope of avoiding the exact details of the where and the why of my location. I didn't want Edmund to feel rejected. Thinking about it, maybe my arrogance was getting the better of me, Edmund has no interest in me, so he can't be jealous, so his feelings would not be hurt if I told him that I was on a date with Gustav.

"I was on a date with Gustav," I said.

Damn it! Sparks smiled knowingly, Edmund gave his cute tilt of the head. I could see him working it out, I hope I didn't hurt his feelings.

"Well, Detective Eager Beaver can finish up here and we can try and salvage our evenings. Edmund, go ahead and I want to talk to Jonathan about when he can write his story," Sparks stated. We both watched Edmund descend the stairs.

Why do I feel like I just got called to the principal's office?

"You know, he has feelings for you," Sparks stated.

"Gustav?" I said confused.

"No, dummy. Edmund. He talks about you quite a bit, more than he has talked about any other person. He loves to talk astronomy, economics, accounting (I could see her eyes roll) and a plethora of other topics. But people, he only talks about you. He hasn't said anything direct like, 'gee, I wish I could date Jonathan,' but I think he does. Be gentle with him, he hurts easily."

Oh god. This can't be true. Just when I had settled on Gustav, Edmund becomes a possibility.

I promised Sparks that I would be super careful with Edmund's feelings; who I date is my choice, but Edmund is still a friend. She also warned me not to just abandon him and run off into the sunset with Gustav. She said my friendship with Edmund means much to him. And if I am honest, it means much to me as well. I'm just not sure how to proceed. If I maintain my friendship with Edmund, I run the risk of further developing those feelings of romance and desire, but if I limit my time with him, it might really hurt him and push him back into his self-isolating shell. And what of Gustav? I don't want to hurt him either. Ugh. Life is hard.

Sunday August 13, 2017

Dear Sam,
After a late night dinner with Gustav, I came back to my apartment alone. It didn't feel right to have him spend the night—not yet. I'm not sure what I am waiting for. He is super perfect. I could tell he would have said yes in a hot, sticky second, but I didn't offer and he didn't push.

As the sun broke through my tiny apartment window, I was alone in my bed, but oddly enough I didn't feel lonely. I felt great about where my relationship with Gustav was headed, I didn't even have any panicky moments of me not being good enough for this German stud. In the handful of meaningful relationships after you, Sam, I never felt like I deserved the man I was dating. Somehow, I always fashioned it that they were better than I was. Smarter, sexier, hipper, it really didn't matter what the attribute, I found something and obsessed over their abundance of it and my lack. Which as you might imagine, doomed the relationship. But this morning, I just was relishing in the restfulness of an early Sunday morning and the prospects of a burgeoning relationship. I got up and made some tea and toast, grabbed the newspaper from outside my door and made it back to the coziness of my bed. I know, who reads a newspaper these days? Well, I do, since I didn't have to pay for it. I had done some writing for the paper a few months back, they gave me a year's free subscription. Oh well, the comics are always worth a look. And who doesn't like a good crossword puzzle?

I pulled the Lifestyle section out first and read the comics. Definitely got a few smiles out of those. Then I started in on the puzzle. Sunday puzzles are usual pretty tough, but proudly I got about a third of the way through it before I got stuck. I was pondering a five-letter word for a bishop's hat when I felt my phone vibrate on the bed. I guess I had put it on silent during my dinner with Gustav last night.

I had 3 missed calls and 5 text messages from Detective Sparks. I read the texts first, starting with the most recent:

Damn it, call me ASAP

This is not good, did you leak this to the paper?

I'm gonna have my ass handed to me by the Captain. I could lose my job over this.

How could you let Edmund talk to a reporter? I told you all of this was off the record.

Did you see the front page of the paper? Did you fucking know about this? Where is Edmund? I can't get a hold of him.

What the hell is going on? I flipped to the front page and in bold, extra big font, a headline read: "Serial Killer Tracked by Police Expert".
Oh shit, oh shit. Not good. Not good.

I read the article and it listed Edmund and Detective Sparks by name and each of the victims' names as well. It discussed the killer's use of Rocuronium Bromide, and quoted Edmund directly. Oh my god. When did Edmund talk to a reporter? Did he know who he was talking to? Who even wrote this? I looked at the byline—Lyman King, of course.

I called Detective Sparks and she screamed at me until I could explain that I knew nothing of this. I told her that Edmund had been at a party with Lyman the weekend before and that's probably where Lyman interviewed Edmund and got all the information.

"Have you heard from Edmund," she asked, "He's not answering any of my calls. I'm getting worried." I told her I hadn't. I called him and after ringing it went to voicemail. I texted him but got no reply. She suggested we go to his apartment to do a "welfare check." Which is Spark's code for "I'm going to find him and kick his ass."

I agreed to meet her at Edmund's to see if we couldn't track him down. On my way out the door, Gustav texted: "Feel like going to a winery today?" Oh my god yes, that would be lovely. But I can't. But once again he loses out in the Edmund-Gustav battle. I called him and explained the situation about the newspaper article and Edmund gone missing. True to form, he offered to help, but I told him that that wasn't necessary. He accepted this without complaint. And ended the call with a "can't wait to see you again." Damn, this German man is scoring all sorts of boyfriend points. Maybe I don't deserve him. Oh look who's back, it's self doubt!

As I drove over to his apartment, my thoughts switched to Edmund. I mulled over where the hell could he be? How does he get himself in such a precarious position? He really is like a puppy. I should've never let him off leash. Maybe I should have chipped him? (Is it legal to chip a human?) Should I put signs up with his picture? When I arrived at Edmund's place fifteen minutes later, Detective Sparks was already there, waiting for me. She looked apocalyptic.

"Have you heard from him," she shouted at me as I got out of my car.

I just shook my head.

We walked into the lobby of his building and knocked on his first floor apartment door. No answer. We checked the parking lot and his car was there. We went back inside the lobby and Sparks knocked again —louder and angrier. (I've often wondered if there is police training on aggressive knocking.) We both were growing more anxious by the minute.

"I think it's warranted; I'm going to break down his door," Sparks declared. She backed up to give herself more room. She readied herself, I cringed a little at the impending noise.

"What are you doing?" said a flat, atonal voice from the doorway of the lobby. It was Edmund.

"Where the hell have you been?" Demanded Sparks in her most serious cop voice.

"Ditto for me," I said in as stern a voice as I could muster. In the stern voice contest, Sparks wins hands down.

Edmund did his cute cock of the head and said, "I was out to brunch with Lyman."

Lyman? Lyman King? Brunch?

I know it's none of my business, but I really couldn't restrain myself. "Edmund, he is not a good guy, you should stay away from him," I warned. Perhaps there was a touch a jealousy in my tone?

"Don't be ridiculous. He is nice," Edmund replied.

Nice? Lyman King? Nice? Maybe nice if he wants something from you, maybe nice until he stabs you in the back, maybe nice until he murders you, your whole family and then murders your whole town...perhaps that last bit is tad hyperbolic.

"I don't care if he was nice, why did you talk to him about the case," Sparks sputtered out through her clenched teeth. Note for Emily: clenched teeth—not a good look for you.

"He seemed really interested and took me seriously. I know the Captain told Jonathan not to publish yet, but I think that the public has a right to know that a serial killer is out there. They need to protect themselves." Edmund reasoned calmly.

"Edmund, not only are you jeopardizing the investigation, you are jeopardizing your work with the police department. They may not hire you again if they see you as someone who can't be trusted with sensitive information," the Detective stated with much less vehemence that I expected.

"Keeping people from being victims of a killer is more important than a job," he said in reply.

My puppy was being logical and making good arguments.

"Edmund, you might even be brought up on charges for hindering an investigation. Additionally, you just made our job harder. The killer now knows that we are on to him. He might change his methods, he will certainly become more careful, and he might even flee." Sparks said with a blend of remonstration and sympathy. At that moment, her cell phone rang. She looked at the number, the way King Louis XVI must have looked at the guillotine. She answered and it and took a few steps away from us.

"Lyman King? Lyman King? I can't believe you, Edmund," I said with just a tad of bitterness.

"He has been very nice to me. I don't understand your problem with him. He didn't make one negative comment about you when I've been around him. He says that he respects you a lot," Edmund responded.

Respects me like a bat respects a baseball...is that even a cogent simile?   Even if it's not, it still counts as a sports analogy.

"Well, I think you should be cautious around him," I softened my tone and tried to at least sound more reasonable. "He can be a fair-weather friend."

"I disagree. He even offered to buy me dinner tonight and wants to talk more about the case," He retorted.

Dinner? Like a date? Is Lyman trying to date my puppy? MY PUPPY?! Go by, mad world! I think my jealousy is getting the better of me. Having thought about it, there is no way Edmund would date Lyman. That is utterly ridiculous.

"Why didn't you answer any of our calls or texts," I demanded.

"Lyman, thought that it would be a good idea to leave my cell phone at home so we wouldn't be disturbed during brunch," Edmund explained.

"Did Lyman leave his cell phone at home?" I asked, already knowing the answer.

"No," he replied simply.

Come on, Edmund. Wake up, Lyman is manipulating you!

At this point, Sparks came back over and told us she had to go back into the station to "deal with the mess that the article has put us in."

She said that the families are furious that they were not told that the news of their loved ones' murders had been made public. And up to this point, the police had not told them that all the murders are linked. "It's going to be weeks of public relations damage control," she lamented.

She reluctantly walked to her car and drove off.

Well, if Edmund was so keen on spending his time with Lyman, I would let him. I have better company, any ways. This felt like betrayal to me. Edmund spending time with Lyman. Maybe it was time to let my puppy go and frolic with whomever he wants. Lyman won this round, he scooped the story and scooped up Edmund. Fine! I know they won't be happy together.

I took my leave of Edmund as brusquely and coldly as I could. He didn't notice. Edmund unlocked his apartment door and went inside. As soon as I got into my car, I texted Gustav saying let's go to that winery and get drunk!

Monday August 14, 2017

Dear Sam,
As you well know, sometimes having sex with someone for the first time can be awkward and unsatisfying. There are expectations and differences in preferences and techniques. There is the pressure to prove your prowess and establish your reputation. Adding in emotional attachment, (anonymous sex is sometimes so much easier), it can be a complete mess.

That was not the case with Gustav. There was exhilaration and comfort. There was passion and tenderness. And then there was a soul-searing orgasm.

Even better, there was the morning after. No rushing about to gather clothes and escape the scene, no awkward regret, no trying to find an excuse to leave, or worse, finding a reason to get them out of your place. We both laid in my bed as the sun streamed through the tiny window in my bedroom. My head snuggled into his broad chest and his arm gently holding me close.

"I'm going to go into work a little late today, if that's ok with you. I'm not quite ready to leave," he cooed quietly to me.

I had no problem at all with that. We lounged in bed for a while longer, in no particular hurry. For all that, the looming reality of our workaday lives eventually forced us to get up. After a late breakfast out, we did finally and reluctantly part, he to his job and me to my apartment to do some writing.

My day was punctuated with texts from him, telling me I was on his mind and suggesting some things we might do under the cover of darkness that would probably shock even the characters in <u>Fifty Shades of Gray</u>. It's getting a little hot in here, isn't it?

Sometimes life gives you a perfect day before the storm rolls in.

Tuesday August 15, 2017

Dear Sam,
Gustav had to work late last before and back in early this morning to catch up for taking yesterday morning off, so we hadn't spent any time together since brunch yesterday. I was occupied in the first part of the day with finishing up a few articles and emailing some editors I know for more work. I got a promising couple of maybes. With the demise of journalism in the last decade, I considered a maybe to be a good thing. I found myself smiling and whistling to myself, and, overall, I had a very productive morning. Having just finished my lunch (a salad and a chocolate chip cookie), my phone dinged.

It was a text from Detective Sparks: "Get to the station ASAP."

Oh, this can't be good, I grabbed my car keys and a second chocolate chip cookie for strength. I arrived shortly with an eerie sense that this was going to turn my good morning into a bad, bad day.

I walked in and an officer ushered me back into a large conference room. Sparks and Edmund were both there as well as Lyman King (I really...well, you know how I feel). There were a dozen other officers and detectives, including the frowsy detective Simmons, seated around an oval table. They were projecting a document on a screen hanging on the wall.

I sidled up next to Sparks who quickly got me up to speed. A letter, addressed to Edmund, had been mailed to the police station and had arrived just a hour or so ago. It was a typed message, printed on seemingly common paper. It purported to be from the serial killer. It read:

My Dearest Edmund,

I was thrilled to read the article in Sunday's paper about my work. I doff my hat to you for figuring out my methodology. I knew the police would never catch on and I am glad that you are someone who could appreciate the efforts I went to. My grandmother always said that like attracts like. But I do wonder if you just got lucky. It is hard to imagine that there is someone out there who can match wits with me. To test this, and you, I've designed some challenges. I will put this is simple terms, so that the cops with you can understand. I will give you clues to my next selection, if you figure it out in time, you can stop me. If you can't figure it out, I win. The cops can consult with all the forensic linguists, hand writing experts, typeologists, phrenologists, criminal psychologists they want, but to no avail. None of those will help them. This is between me and you (you can bring along your reporter sidekick, as you like). I can't tell you how thrilled I am to be able to play this little game with you. I should warn you that anyone who is playing in our contest is fair game. When I defeat you, I'm going to drink in this victory and it'll be sweet. It's a shame that we have to be opponents; in a different reality I could have called you friend.

—Tarkshya

Ps. This red   diamond is our little way to know if a letter is from me.

I would hate for someone else to take credit for my work.

 Some people in the past have called me self-absorbed. Maybe that is not unwarranted since my first thought was feeling insulted for being called a sidekick. Really, I'm just a sidekick? Wow, that's a blow to my ego. I guess the more socially acceptable thing would be to focus on that this guy is planning on killing more people just to beat Edmund in a game of wits. Now that I think of it, I might not be the sidekick, the sidekick might refer to Lyman who actually wrote the article that blew this whole thing up. Ugh, to be lumped in with Lyman, that just adds insult to injury.

The conversation around the conference room was buzzing. Everyone seemed to have a theory about who this guy was and how best to analyze the letter. Only two people were quiet, Edmund and the police captain—John Horace Burleson. The captain was in his early sixties with a squarish face and sharp eyes. He had been working on the police force for more than 35 years. It looked like he was lost in thought and oblivious to the bedlam around him, but I knew better. He was organizing his strategy. I had interviewed him a few times over the years and knew he played his cards close to his vest (does this count as a sports analogy—they do show poker on ESPN). I watched him for a few minutes wondering when he would rein in this chaos.

After a while, he slowly stood up and the room fell silent, all eyes were on him (except Edmund's, he was still staring at the letter).

"All right, we have an advantage over this maniac. We know that, like most serial killers, he is narcissistic and from his letter, he thinks he is smarter than us, let's prove him wrong. First, I want hair, fingerprint and DNA analysis on the letter and envelope. Figure out where this letter was mailed from. And, I do want linguistic analysis and a criminal profile made on this pyscho despite the fact he said that it won't help us. It just might. Edmund, I am sure you picked up on the fact that he is threatening your life, so I want to put you in protective custody." The captain said.

"That won't be necessary," Edmund replied calmly, "He wants to toy with me rather than kill me. He would be more likely to go after people I care about." He glanced at me.

What? He cares about me. After our fight Sunday? Well, knowing Edmund, he didn't realize we even had a fight.

"Who do you think the 'reporter sidekick' refers to? Mr. King or Mr. Somers?" He asked Edmund.

"Here I think he is being clever. I am sure that he is referring to both. He wants to cause confusion. I think it gives him a sense of power when other people are struggling and helpless. That's his whole methodology," Edmund stated still staring at the letter. The Captain, following his eyes, reread the note.

"What's a phrenologist?" The captain wondered.

"Someone who measures the bumps on a person's head to determine their personality. It is a pseudo-science that has been long discredited," Edmund replied dismissively.

"Does his name mean anything?" Burleson asked.

"It comes from Hindu mythology. It a mythical being often described as a horse or a bird." Edmund replied in a distracted way. "Other than that, I don't see any significance to it."

I could tell that during this conversation with Captain Burleson, Edmund was still analyzing the letter. I was watching him closely and saw his eyes dart from one part of the letter to another. It was as if he was organizing it into some mental spreadsheet.

Sparks spoke up, "Did anyone else here notice he misspelled 'typologist?'"

I didn't. I'm a terrible speller. Thank god for spell-check!

A few of the detectives nodded in agreement.

"Do you think it's just a typo or was it intentional?" One of the officers asked.

"Definitely intentional, this man, or should I say person, though the vast majority of serial killers are men. I will keep using the masculine pronoun for the sake of clarity. Anyways, he is very careful, he won't make many mistakes," Edmund said without taking his eyes off the letter. I could almost see the gears of his mind moving.

"If what you say is true, Edmund, it's going to be tough catching him." Sparks stated.

Edmund shot her a look that clearly said, "Of course, what I say is true."

"I think Edmund is right, this guy is not going to make many mistakes, so that means we need to not make many ourselves. By the book, people, no slip-ups," commanded Burleson.

"Can everyone leave so I can process this...everyone except Jonathan?" His tone was typically Edmund, direct and without much emotion. But know him as I did, I could tell he was rankled and distracted by all the commotion. It was clear that the officers didn't want to take an order from him, and looked to the Captain for direction. He himself was clearly irked at having a civilian give an order, but realized that this was probably a good idea.

"Okay, we have things to do. Let's get on this," the captain gave the order and the officers in the room dispersed by twos and threes. Lyman was unsure whether he should go or stay.

"Edmund, do you want me to stay?" He asked sweetly. Get the hell out you snake!

"No," was Edmund's only reply. Lyman left with a sneer at me. I smiled broadly at him.

I sat silently next to Edmund. His fingers worked on the air in front of him as if he were sliding pieces in a puzzle. From time to time, he would google something or another on his phone. He did this for many minutes, but I knew better than to interrupt him with my inane questioning.

"He didn't give me all the pieces," Edmund finally said. "I can't solve this. And he knows it. I have to go out to find the rest of this puzzle. But where?"

I know the letter contained lots of clues and I know I had no idea how to make sense of them. I asked Edmund to explain what he meant.

"He's giving me clues to a location, but also a lot of superfluous detail. His grandmother is a red herring, the phrenologist—red herring, the red diamond—red herring. But there is not enough detail here to make a determination."

"You can't figure it out?" I was disappointed.

"No, you are not listening to me. I can figure it out if all the pieces were there, but he has intentionally withheld a piece. I'm not sure why," Edmund explained curtly.

"It is because he wants to beat you and gloat?" I suggested.

"No, more than that, he wants a challenge, that's the reason for letter. He wants to prove he is the smartest, so he is going up against the smartest person the police have—me." Edmund said this without a sense of boasting—to him, it was just a fact.

We lapsed into silence; once again, I was unsure of how I could help him. Maybe just me sitting with him helped. Unfortunately, I was not great at sitting by and doing nothing. For a while, I resisted my Pavlovian urge to pull out my phone and scroll through social media. But my will power isn't all that strong, just as I was reaching into my pocket, Edmund broke the silence.

"Interesting, he hasn't yet given me the final piece to this puzzle. Was it to give himself more time to implement his plan?" I hoped this was a rhetorical question, because I had no idea. Thankfully, he answered his own question. "He must have rushed to get all this together. It's only been two days since the article was published. He was so eager to play that he could not stop himself from mailing this before he had worked out all the details. He's going to deliver the last piece of this puzzle, but how? And when? He's not going to mail it, it must be more immediate. On the news? No, too overt. It'll be more subtle."

Suddenly, Edmund stood up and rushed out of the room and I followed (maybe I am the sidekick). He approached Detective Sparks. "I need to see a list of 911 calls made in the last two or three hours. I'm looking for something weird or unusual." Again, his asking is really more like demanding.

My puppy needs to learn manners.

Sparks took a couple minutes to figure out what Edmund was really asking for. Eventually, she led us to the 911 dispatch room and asked one of the operators to bring up a list of recent calls. The operator read down the list.

"Domestic dispute"
"Lost dog"

"Pick pocket"

"How about an escaped boa constrictor?" He asked.

"No, the killer would never work with animals. Too unpredictable." Edmund replied.

"Except for a murderous bovine," I said under my breath.

"That's about it, it's been a slow afternoon, thankfully." The 911 operator stated.

"Tell me about the pick pocket," Edmund commanded.

"Um, a 43 year old woman called to say that her wallet was taken out of her purse while she was shopping at Target. Oh, here's an odd detail, and the woman said the thief left a black walnut in her purse." The operator said after a quizzical look to Sparks, who just shrugged her shoulders.

Edmund's eyes darted back and forth for a moment, then went wide. "Of course," he uttered. He ran back into the conference room.

Sparks and I exchanged looks, both of us not seeing what Edmund did. But we followed him. He was seated at the table furiously working on his iPhone. After a few moments, he held it up so we could see. It was open to the website of the Yellow Cab Cafe, a local bar known for being an arts venue and hosting a weekly poetry slam. I've been there a few times myself, it's a great place.

"We have to call them immediately and warn them that their patrons are in danger. The killer is likely to poison one or more of them," Edmund barked at us.

Slow down, puppy.

"How do you know this?" I beat Sparks to this question by half a breath.

Edmund sighed a sigh of exasperation, to him it was obvious. "The misspelling of typology was an obvious reference to the type or font of the letter. It took me a bit to find out that the font name is Yellow Ginger. But I didn't know what to do with that, there were too many possibilities. The killer had to deliver more information before anyone could solve this, that's when I thought of the 911 calls. He knew the police would have that information and therefore I would have access to it. The pickpocket stole a wallet from a woman's purse and replaced it with a black walnut. I did a quick google search for "yellow" and "walnut" and found out that this bar, The Yellow Cab, is on Walnut Street. Additionally, as everyone knows, that black walnuts poison other plants around them. Hence, he is going to poison someone with a ginger drink at the Yellow Cab. Now, call them and warn them." He handed his phone to Sparks.

She brushed it aside and got out her own. She stepped out of the conference room to have officers dispatched and to make the call to the bar.

"Edmund, you were brilliant. I can't believe you pieced that all together. You deserve a medal! (Or a puppy treat!)" I exclaimed. I put my hand on his shoulder in a friendly manner. He pulled away from me. I had forgotten he doesn't like to be touched.

Edmund resumed his study of the letter and I just hung out next to him (yes, like a sidekick). For several long minutes, Edmund stared unmoving. I fidgeted like a kid during the marshmallow test.

Detective Sparks re-entered the room. "We might be too late, a patron at the bar collapsed just before I called. They are rushing him to the hospital now. I've sent some officers ahead of us, but I am not sure that this is the work of our guy, but we'll go there and see what the witnesses have to say," Sparks said.   She grabbed her keys and headed out to the parking lot.

"So, you beat this guy! Edmund, that is incredible," I crooned. "So, does this mean he'll stop trying to kill people now that he is defeated?"

Sparks did her Spock eyebrow thing.

"That would be an unreasonable conclusion," Edmund stated. "I think Detective Sparks would agree that this person is unlikely to stop until he is caught or killed."

"What he said," Sparks replied as she unlocked her department issued car, more aptly to be described as a jalopy. I did just now spend several minutes googling slang words for a dilapidated car. There was quite the selection, but I think jalopy works for my purposes. It was rust covered, dented and dinged, the left rear passenger window was cracked and there were several missing parts, but not being a car guy, I can't really tell you what parts they were.

Reluctantly, I got into the Detective's car and we sped off to the Yellow Cab Cafe. In no time at all, we arrived at the bar; it was just a few blocks away from the station. The police had taped off the bar already, a few curious onlookers milled about, but no news media were there yet. She ushered us past the uniformed officer and into the bar.

The bar's owner, a tall, slim man in his mid-forties and the bartender, a twenty-something woman with absolutely flawless skin exquisitely decorated with colorful tattoos, both were being questioned by Detective Simmons who quickly caught us up. The poisoning, if that was what it was, took place just after the lunch rush. There had only been one customer drinking at the bar, the victim; a few other people had come in for some late lunch carryout orders. The customer ordered his usual, he was a regular, a quiet guy in his late sixties. Everything was normal until the guy passed out and fell onto the floor.

Edmund's only question: "What was he drinking?"

Sparks looked a bit stunned. Even with all her experience being around Edmund, his lack of social grace still threw her.

"Is it that important right now?" Simmons asked, clearly irked.

"Very," Edmund replied with surprise.

"It's called an Apple Ginger Stonewall Cocktail," The bartender said.

"I've never heard of that before and I know my way around a bar." Sparks whispered, more to herself and then was slightly chagrined; she probably said more than she wanted to. No worries though, it was lost on Edmund and it would be hypocritical of me to judge someone for being a fan of alcohol; me and alcohol are old, old friends.

"Why does the name of the drink matter, Edmund?" I asked.

"With this perpetrator, everything matters. The more information I have, the more likely I am to predict his actions and solve his puzzles. We may not have stopped him this time, but we will next time by understanding how he thinks and this will be accomplished by studying the patterns of his behaviors and words," Edmund stated matter-of-factly. It really wasn't about ego with him, he just perceives that his idea is the right one. And often it is.

"You said 'next time,' are you sure he will continue?" I said apprehensively.

"There is no doubt he will continue. These killings give his life meaning, this is the most important thing in his life," he replied. He words sent a chill up my spine.

Sparks led us away from Simmons and the witnesses, so we could more freely discuss Edmond's ideas.

"What does the name of the drink tell you?" I asked my follow-up question.

"Nothing by itself, but if we add details from the letter to it, it tells us a great deal. This letter is written for me and about me. First, the quote from his grandmother, "like attracts like," his phrase at the end of his letter, "In a different reality, I could have called you friend," and the name of the drink all tell me he thinks I'm gay. The Stonewall Riots in New York started the modern movement for gay rights." Edmund explained.

Was he about to come out to us? I love watching people come out! Damn, I wish I had some rainbow confetti.

"Why would he let you know the he thinks you're gay? Are you saying he is homophobic?" Sparks asked.

"Perhaps, but I think it more to unnerve me. He thinks I might feel threatened by his intimate knowledge of me. But I am not unnerved." Edmund stated with usual flat affect. "I am sure there is more significance to the quote about "in a different reality, I could have called you friend," but I don't recognize it." He admitted with a tinge of shame.

Sparks looked at me and then Edmund expectantly. I certainly had no idea.

"You guys never watched Star Trek? This is from one the original episodes, a real classic. A Romulon commander says this to Captain Kirk just before he kills himself after a grueling space battle. It's one of the great ones," Sparks boldly stated.

Oh, an alcoholic Trekkie, very chic, Detective Sparks.

"What was the name of the character who said the line?" Edmund asked.

"He didn't have a name, he was known as the Romulon commander." Sparks said.

"What was the name of the actor who said the line?" Edmund inquired.

"Mark Lenard, I think," Sparks replied. Again we looked at her, how does she know this? "I do a lot of bar trivia." She said with a bashful grin.

We all were just pondering this information trying to make sense of it, when Sparks realized that she should go and see if the bar had any surveillance video.

Edmund lapsed into his characteristic silence, staring at nothing. And I tossed about for something to hold my attention. I began thinking about his comment about the killer thinking he was gay. I was bummed that he didn't come out...as anything. What does he self-identify as? Is that area of his life not important? Maybe, he had never given it much thought. Maybe, it's none of my business. But I so want to know!

To distract myself, I was casually looking over a bulletin board of poems that some patrons had written and tacked up. Some were typical bar poems, silly, obscene, clever, but some were very well written. Then something caught my eye:

It was in the corner of one of the poems.

It read:

I met a man on the way from the Zoo
He had so many animals, he didn't know what to do:
Four horses, a dog and two cats,
A dozen elephants and three bats,
Five zebras with stripes black and white,
Two lions spoiling for a flight,

A dove with a hawthorn sprig,
And three of the cutest little pigs,
It was lucky and fortunate for us two meet
Their journey was to end with so many feet.

"Edmund, I think I found something," I squealed in excitement loud enough for Sparks to hear.

Both Edmund and Sparks rushed over. I pointed to the red diamond at the bottom of the page. They both read the poem, but Edmund spoke first.

"It's referencing the Wright Brothers' first flight," he announced.

What? I think I got whiplash from my head snap!

"Edmund, that's ridiculous, how can you know that?" Sparks stated.

Sparks is about to be schooled by my puppy—I love it when he does this!

"Notice that he has misused two words "flight" and "two," the phrase should read "spoiling for a fight" but instead he uses the word "flight." In the second to last line, he uses "two" when grammatically it should be "to." He is calling attention to something that is a pair. Two and flight lead me to the Wright Brothers, as well as the hawthorn sprig reference, Hawthorn, that's the name of the street they lived on here in Dayton. Additionally, if you add up the number of feet from all the animals (and the man going to the zoo) it equals 120 feet, the distance of their first flight. This leads me to the sculpture downtown that represents their first flight, though the sculpture itself is only 110 feet long, I don't really know why when all the sources I've read..."

My puppy likes to ramble. But I cut him off, "Shouldn't we go?"

Sparks was already on the radio asking for officers to reroute traffic away from that sculpture. We loaded into the Detective's car and raced over to Main Street where the sculpture is located. We were one of the first police cars there. A few officers had started to divert traffic away from the piece of art. Edmund took a few steps towards the sculpture, but Sparks grabbed his arm.

"You can't go near that until we've checked it out, to make sure it's safe," Sparks warned him.

"That's absurd, he's a killer, not a bomber," Edmund said exasperated.

"Stay!" She commanded. Maybe she thinks of him as a puppy as well.

Reluctantly, he stayed. She and several other officers began a search of the sculpture. During his wait, Edmund scanned the crowds that had gathered to watch the police action. He said that the perpetrator would likely be in the crowd to watch the chaos he caused. After a while, a bomb sniffing dog team showed up. But after going around the sculpture a couple of times, the dog had no reaction—meaning no bombs were there. I heard Edmund mutter under his breath, "I already knew that."

After many long minutes, Sparks called us over.
"It's clean as far as we can tell," the detective said. "But we did find this." She held up a mostly completed Sudoku. Nine numbers were missing and there was a tiny red diamond at the bottoms of the page.

"2, 2, 3, 5, 6, 7, 8, 8, 8." Edmund rattled off after about seven and half seconds.
Sparks and I looked at him expectantly. Edmund just looked back.

"Well..." Sparks said.

"Well what?" Edmund retorted.

"What do the numbers mean?" She hissed through her teeth. Again, not a good look for Sparks.

"I have no idea," Edmund replied calmly. How can this be? He never fails.

"You need more time to figure it out?" I prompted.

"No," Edmund lapsed into silence. We had made such progress and now he has reverted back to his monosyllabic phase.

"Why can't you figure it out?" Sparks again hissed through her clenched jaw. Not to be nibby, but clenched jaw—not doing any favors to her appearance.

"No one can figure it out. The killer didn't provide enough information again. These nine numbers could mean anything. It could a social security number, it could be part of a substitution cypher, or an Internet address. There's no way to know until he provides us with more information," Edmund explained.

"Well, this is where good old fashion police works saves the day," Sparks touted. "We have guys that can run these numbers through analysis software and look at different possibilities. We might get lucky."

Thankfully, Edmund chose not to comment.

Detective Simmons came over and pulled Sparks away for a private conversation. I got the distinct feeling that the trench coat toting Simmons did not think much of Edmund and his talent. He kept throwing dirty looks at us.

There wasn't much more for us to do at the scene until we got more information. Out of habit, I asked Edmund if he wanted to grab some dinner (Sparks was going home to hang with the fiancé). He declined —no surprise. Then he said he was having dinner with Lyman—yes surprise.

"Oh," I said. "How..how's that going?" Whatever THAT was.

"Good," he replied with his supercilious eyebrow. "He really likes to listen to my stories. He is going to buy me dinner again."

Ugh...to be honest, it's not any of my business, but that's never, ever stopped me before.

"Edmund, I want you to be careful. Lyman, may not have your best interest at heart." I warned as gently as I could.

He did his puppy dog cock of the head. And then he just walked away.

Jonathan 2—Lyman 400. Nothing left to do but hit the showers— with Gustav! (Yea! Another sports reference.)

Sunday August 20, 2017

Dear Sam,

Tonight, we had Detective Sparks and her fiancé over for cocktails and tapas. He's a nice guy—her fiancé. His name is Daniel M'Cumber, a salesman for some solar power company. Thankfully, he didn't talk about his job too much. He and Gustav hit it off rather well, talking about some of the places they both have travelled to. Whereas, Emily and I discussed the case. She summed it up pretty well: It had been five days and nothing new from the killer as far as we knew. Sparks also told me that the police analysts haven't had any luck analyzing the Sudoku numbers. They also have struck out with tracking down the where the killer got the Rocuronium Bromide, and even the fingerprints and DNA has told them little. They were 18 different DNA profiles found on the original letter and none of them led to any viable suspect. There were more than two dozen sets of fingerprints lifted from the paper and envelope, including a set that was traced back to Nancy Cartwright (ay caramba) of all people. The security footage from the Yellow Cab Cafe provided nothing; their system had not been working for the last few couple weeks.

"We have one last avenue of technical investigation," Sparks explained. "Are you familiar with something called Machine Identification Code?"

I shook my head no.

"Every printer leaves nearly invisible dots on every page it prints. Those dots can be used to identify which printer printed a page," Sparks stated. "Assuming, he hasn't figured a way around that. He's been one step ahead of us this whole time."

"He has indeed," I said. "Are you going to test every printer in the city? That shouldn't take but a decade or so."

"No, but we can use that to rule a suspect in or out." Sparks explained.

"Any update on the man who was poisoned at the Yellow Cab?"

"Thankfully, he'll make a full recovery. Edmund saved his life, by telling the ER that he had been poisoned, it saved a lot of time tracking down what caused his collapse. Edmund, figuring out all those clues, I have never met anyone like him." She mused, then glancing over to Gustav and Daniel. "Looks like our men are getting along."

I looked over at Gustav and saw that he was showing Daniel pics from his hometown. I smiled at the domesticity of this moment. It felt good. Then, as usual, I went and did something to undermine the happy mood.

"How's Edmund doing?" I asked Emily quietly.

"He's working hard," Emily replied. "There seems to be no end of work for him, unrelated to our case. Though Captain Burleson did have a little heart to heart with about how and when to speak to the media. The Captain is more bark than bite, but that day he barked quite a lot."

"But personally, how is he doing?" Why do I do this? Can't I not poke the bear?

Emily paused. She seemed reluctant to answer.

"He is spending a lot of time with Lyman King." She raised a hand to silence my protest. "I know you don't like him. He needs this socialization but I'm not sure that Lyman is always looking out for Edmund's best interest. This is not a very balanced relationship. I can't really tell if they are dating in the traditional sense, there is little about Edmund that falls under the "traditional" category. He talks about Lyman a lot, whereas before he talked about you." Ouch, Sparks launched a guilt dart. "He mentions how Lyman has helped him pick out a new wardrobe."

"Well, the man does need a fashion mentor," I replied.

"He has also said that Lyman has encouraged him to take on less police work and more private clients. "

"Ok, that's not the worst thing that can happen," I said with a bit of uncertainty.

"Jonathan, he has said that Lyman wants him to go after the serial killer by himself—without the police," Sparks said in hushed tones. "Lyman couches it in terms of how great he is and that the police are holding him back with unnecessary procedures and protocols. You know how Edmund is, he can't tell honest praise from insincere flattery. What if Lyman is setting him up to in order to get the story on the serial killer? Is Lyman that ambitious?"

"Ambitious isn't a word I would use to describe Lyman, that implies hard work." I replied. "But he will take advantage of situations and people. He might be buttering Edmund up to get the scoop on this story. A story like this could really get his name out there; it might even make national headlines. This could skyrocket Lyman's career. Have you said anything to Edmund about this yet?"

"Not directly. I was hoping you could steer him clear of Lyman. I keep bringing up you and if he has seen or heard from you. He hasn't." She said those last two words with emphasis. "Remember, I said you couldn't just abandon him." Another guilt dart. "You have been the only person he has reached out to. You are significant in his life, no matter what Lyman does." She speaks directly, doesn't she? "You haven't contacted him since last week, have you?" A trifecta of guilt darts. Well done, Sparks, well done.

"No," I replied looking down at my drink. "But I will, tomorrow, I pinky promise."

I took a long slow slip of my cocktail. Sparks, wanting to relieve the tension, asked me what was it that I was drinking.

"It's called a Juanita More. I first had it two years ago when I was in the City by the Bay (San Francisco) for Pride. It's a mix of blackberries, lemon, Jameson, bitters and ginger beer. It's a little fruity and a little spicy—remind you of anybody? I batted my eyelashes at her.

Now it was her turn to roll her eyes.

Monday August 21, 2017

Dear Sam,

Being the good friend, I texted Edmund. To my surprise, he asked if we could meet after work for some tea. There's a great little place downtown, Ghostlight Coffee, that he suggested we meet. He was there ahead of me and had ordered (and paid for) a tea for me. I know right, I was shocked too. He was wearing some of his new clothes, a sharply blue dress shirt with a geometrically patterned tie and some off-white khakis. I must admit, Lyman has good taste—ONLY when it comes to clothes. I, of course, was fashionably dressed as well—my furiously cleaned skinny jeans and a black and white sleeveless hoodie.

I greeted him and asked how he was.

"I'm doing well, but there has been no word from the killer..." he began. I held up a hand to stop him. We were in a crowded place and it probably wouldn't be wise to openly discuss a serial killer.

"Let's call him 'our friend,'" I suggested.

Clearly, Edmund thought this unnecessary but agreed.

"As I was saying, our friend has not made contact with anyone. It's been nearly a week. I keep thinking, I might have missed something." This didn't sound like the Edmund I know. "Lyman thinks I must have missed a clue. He has made me go over and over all the data. I believe I have been thorough and I don't think I missed anything. But Lyman insists I did."

"You are doubting yourself?" I was incredulous.

"I didn't think our friend would wait this long before giving us the next step. Maybe he did, and I didn't see it." He lapsed into a doubtful silence which was also rather uncharacteristic of him. I don't think Lyman is helping his self-esteem.

"Do you want to go over everything again to see what we can shake loose?" I offered.

"No, that's not why I asked to meet with you. I need some advice about Lyman," he replied.

Okay...that's different. We are boldly going where no man has gone before—damn it Sparks, you got me quoting Star Trek!

"Sure, I'll be happy to help," I said with a forced smiled.

"You may not have realized this but I am gay and earlier this summer I thought I wanted to date you, but then you met Gustav. That got me thinking that I should get some dating experience and Lyman expressed interest, so I accepted his invitation." It all sounded so clinical.

In college, I was part of an improv group (the Dorknobs) and I consider myself a pretty good actor, but having to sit across from Edmund and discuss his romantic relationship with Lyman King was the greatest performance of my life. My feelings for Edmund haven't really died out but have become dormant and superseded by my feelings for Gustav, and my hatred for Lyman has always been frothing just under the surface, or truth be told, bubbling up for all to see. I really wanted to both hug him and hit him—trying to knock some sense into him. If the conversation turned to problems in the bedroom, I improvised a plan on the spot—I was going to fake a heart attack.

He started to describe his relationship and why he felt he needed experience. After too much, way too much superfluous detail, he finally got to his question.

"How does one know when one is in love?" He asked without emotion, just another curious google search to him.

"That's a tough question," I replied. "Love is very complicated and comes in many forms. True love, romantic love, blind love, puppy love." I paused at the joke I made, but realized I have never told him that I think of him as a little dog. "Edmund, it is easy to mistake sexual drive or the desire to be with someone as love, but love is a balanced thing that both people give equally to."

"I am not engaging in a sexual relationship with Lyman," He stated flatly with just a touch of disgust. I felt that heart attack coming on.

"Ok, tell me why you think you are in love with Lyman." I asked, digging a little deeper.

"You misunderstand me, I am not in love with Lyman. He says he is in love with me. I think that this is premature. Certainly, one cannot fall in love with someone having known them but a few weeks." He implemented his supercilious eyebrow.

"Generally, that's true. But there can be exceptions to that." I explain. "But I agree with you, I don't think Lyman is truly in love with you." I added quickly, oh so quickly.

"Thank you. I needed that confirmation. I don't have much experience dating and I am forced to rely on your vast experience." Vast? Vast? I don't have vast dating experience: one guy in high school, three or four in college (or five or six or a dozen...that's not the point.). I might have had several short term liaisons since college, and of course you, Sam, but I would never describe it as vast. I thought about warning Edmund that my "vast" experience hasn't amounted to much. Just a lot of heartache, lonely nights and a few

(few being a relative term) regrettable short-term, late night app-initiated rendezvous (or is the plural rendezvi?). But now I have Gustav, I am not sure what I have done to have this kind of deep and meaningful relationship, but it is on a whole different plane than anything before—there's only one relationship that I've been in that rivaled this, Sam.

At this point, a cute Twinkie barista came over and put a blueberry muffin down in front of Edmund. It had a plastic cartoon character sticking out of top of it.

"I didn't order this," Edmund stated bluntly.

"The gentlemen over there asked me to deliver this to you," the barista pointed back to the bar. We all turned our heads to see this man. "Huh, he's gone." The cute, but garden variety twink, made duck lips in his confusion and turned away.

"Wait," I called him back (not just to get a second look at him), "Do you sell these cartoon plastics things" I pointed to the muffin topper.

"No, that man brought it with him and asked me to stick it in. He said you would understand." Again, the young man pursed his lips as he tried to comprehend this perplexing situation.

"Edmund, don't touch it. There might be fingerprints or DNA on it." I said as he reached for it. I looked closely at it and recognized it as one of Donald Duck's nephews.

"I wonder which nephew this is," I said under my breath.

The barista, still standing there, replied, "It's Dewey, he always wears blue." And with that he sauntered away.

Damn Disney loving twink.

"Jonathan, look." Edmund pointed to small red diamond drawn on Dewey's ass.

"I think our friend just made contact with you." I announced.

We called Sparks immediately and she dispatched a team over to interview the employees and customers, as well as gather evidence from the muffin. Unfortunately, the coffee shop did not have security cameras.

"Why this duck?" I asked Edmund.

"I'm sure it's the name that's important, but not sure what it is referencing," Edmund said.

"There's a Dewey's pizza over on Brown Street," I offered.

"No, I don't think that's it. It should help us make sense of his last clue: the Sudoku we found at the First Flight sculpture." He paused in thought, "The name Dewey and a bunch of numbers: the Dewey Decimal System. He's referencing a book." He excitedly (for Edmund) stated.

"To the book depository!" Edmund just stared at me. No one ever gets my Simpsons' references. Sigh.

"We can just search online for the book," Edmund logically explained.

"I don't remember all the numbers," I lamented. "Let's ask Sparks, I'm sure she made a note."

"2, 3, 3, 5, 5, 6, 7, 9." Edmund recites from memory.

"Ok, that's a lot of digits for a book number." I tell him.

"It is likely the book and page number. Most Dewey Decimal notations are a three digit number followed by a decimal point then two or three more numbers. 233.556, for example. The last two digits would represent the book page, in our case, 79." Edmund explains as he types the number into the city's library database.

"Well, what's the book?" I prompted him.

He found it on his phone and pondered its significance. "It is a book on Christian Theology called The Divinity Code to Understanding Your Dreams and Visions. I'll see if I can find a pdf and download it."

"Edmund, that's not going to work. I think we have to go to the library itself and find this book. He can't inscribe a red diamond on a website." I instructed.

"Perhaps, you're right." He admitted. I thought for sure he was going to argue that one can place a red diamond on website, but I'm glad he didn't. And let me just say, Edmund said I was right. That's a glittery gold star for me.

As we got up from our table, the good detective Sparks arrived with her legions of police. We told her what we have found and the three of us raced off to the library, which was only a couple of blocks away. Sparks didn't even have time to turn on her sirens. Just a quick side note, I thought the police were supposed to be trained in good driving, perhaps Sparks needs a refresher course and I might have needed some Tums. When we arrived, we quickly found our book with the help of the librarian du jour. Edmund hurriedly turned to page 79 and laid it flat on a table to reveal nothing. No red diamond, no note, no drawing, no cryptic clue. Nothing. We shook the book out, we looked on the shelves around it, nothing.

I pointed out the the exact book number is 233.55, no 6 on the end. We decided to check on page 67 just in case. The book only had 112 pages, so the page number couldn't be 679. We checked to see if there is a book with 233.556 as its book number, no luck.

"How did we get this wrong?" Sparks asked.

"I'm not sure," Edmund numbly replied.

"The numbers you read off the Sudoku page were in that order?" I inquired.

"No, I put them in numerical order to better organize them," Edmund answered, his eyes going slightly wide at his mistake.

"What was the original order," I asked getting rather excited. I might have actually helped on this one!

"Uh, 6, 3, 7, 3, 5, 2, 5, 9." Edmund recalled with some minor difficulty. He might be more rattled by this puzzle than I thought. Or is it his relationship with Lyman that had him distracted? It certainly is distracting me, well, nauseating me would be more like it. I had the same feeling as when I watched the scene where Jabba the Hutt licked Leia in Return of the Jedi. Shiver.

We raced over to the 600s. This section, among other things, contained books about food. We found the one with the book number 637.35 The World Cheese Book. Sparks opened the book to page 259 (it was a damn big book) and we immediately spotted a small red diamond drawn on the bottom of page. The featured cheese on that page was called Negroni. It's an Italian cheese.

"Yes! We are going to Italy," I squealed out. Several library patrons turned to look and shake their heads in disapproval.

"We are not going to Italy," Sparks insisted with that tone of voice that implies an eye roll. "So far, our killer has confined his activities within the bounds of the city limits. There is no reason to think he has taken flight to Europe."

Damn, I could really use a trip to Italy, especially on the police department's dime.

"Let's see if anyone local sells this cheese," Edmund suggested. He worked his magic on his iPhone. "There's only one cheese shop within the city limits, Crafted and Cured. But it is already closed for the night. Detective Sparks, you can break in legally."

"No, I cannot. We need to get a warrant but that will take hours. We might as well wait until they open in the morning." She stated.

"No. Someone's life may be in danger. We must act now." Edmund demanded.

She sighed. But eventually began to make calls. I decided to take a few pics of the page in the World Cheese Book. You never know, we might need more information from this page.

Edmund had picked up a random book off a shelf and was perusing it. Then his phone rang with its prosaic ring. He answered it, but I only heard his half of the conversation.

"Yes, a clue led us to the downtown library. Yes, I'm working on it right now."

"No, you cannot join me. Captain Burleson made it clear that you cannot be at an active crime scene."

"Yes, he's here."

"You are being ridiculous. He has never "made a move" on me. (He did the single-handed air quotes).

A long pause—I could not hear what the other party was saying.

"I discussed that with Jonathan and he agrees with me that you are not really in love with me."

"WHAT THE HELL? YOU DISCUSSED OUR PRIVATE RELATIONSHIP WITH HIM?!" I heard that.

"Call me back when you can be rational." Edmund concluded the conversation in his usual brusque manner.   I almost, *almost* felt sorry for Lyman.

Sparks came over to us and said that she tracked down the shop owner and he has agreed to meet us at his cheese shop.

A grumpy looking man with a handlebar mustache was waiting for us outside the Crafted and Cured shop. He was a bit confused as to what we were looking for.

"Have you had any odd customer interactions in the last couple days?" Sparks asked.

"Nothing I can think of," was his reply.

"Have you seen a small red diamond on anything, a piece of paper, a corkscrew, a wheel of cheese?"

"No..." the shopkeeper said with a pause. "But diamond sounds familiar." He searched through some receipts. "Here, a Reed Diamond placed a phone order yesterday. He said somebody would come by today and pick it up, but no one did." He handed us a circular brown paper bag with a cheese tray inside. Attached to the bag, was a note which was addressed to Edmund.

Dearest Edmund,

I have been watching your love Triangle with interest. I wood have thought that our paths had crossed already, but for now, I'll be hanging out with Paul Stamets and Hugh Culber discussing symbols of the Underworld.

Reed Diamond

"The word Triangle refers to Triangle Park just north of downtown." Edmund stated. "But I have no idea who Paul Stamets and Hugh Culber are."

For some reason Sparks looked a little embarrassed.

"Do you know who these people are?" I asked.

"Yes," She said reluctantly, "Next month, a new Star Trek series will debut and those two are characters from the show."

Oh great, more Star Trek.

"Don't judge me. I've really been looking forward to this series and have read everything I could find about it online." Sparks defended herself. "And, it might interest you that they are the first gay couple in any Star Trek series."

"Okay, we need to look for gays in Triangle park. And here, I thought my days of cruising the parks were over." I replied snarkily.

"I'm sure that's not what our friend means," Sparks retorted. "At least I hope not."

"What more can you tell me about these characters?" Edmund asked.

"Well, Paul is an engineer and Hugh is a doctor. That's about all I know. They've kept a tight lid on the show." She explained.

"That doesn't seem to be much use," Edmund bluntly stated. "Is the show set on the Enterprise?"

"No, the ship is called the Discovery," Sparks is just full of Trek trivia.

"The Boonshoft Museum of Discovery is in Triangle Park!" Edmund blurted out.

Sparks radioed for all units to head that way. The sun was just about to set when we arrived. About half a dozen police cars were there by time we pulled into the parking lot. Individual officers were fanning out and searching the grounds. The museum had been closed for several hours and the parking lot was nearly deserted but for a few cars of the night staff and a couple of construction vehicles for the ongoing renovation.

We raced up the step to the main entrance where Detective Simmons was already pounding on the glass front entrance (how does he always get to the scene first?).

The four of us waited as the world's slowest janitor made his slow, slow way to door. Both detectives were showing their badges and this guy still said, "The museum is closed."

"Sir, this is the police. Open the door, it's an emergency." Sparks said in her most commanding police voice. I wonder if she ever uses that voice with her fiancé in the bedroom. Oy, what a thought, bad Jonathan, bad, bad Jonathan!

The janitor looked from Sparks to Simmons, back to Sparks. What was this guy waiting for? While we were standing there, it literally went from day to night and the museum's outside lighting came on. Then we heard one the officers cry out, "Detectives, over here!"

We raced down the front steps and around a corner of the building where we found the officer and we followed his gaze up to the roof. On top the museum's observatory tower, was a man tied to a wooden frame. He looked dead.

"How do we get up there? See if there is access around the back of the building," Sparks told her officers. Several began the long run around the extensive building. "Can you hear me, I'm with the police and we are here to help!" She shouted up to the bound man.

There was no response at first, but after half a minute the man moved his head and uttered a low moan.

"Oh my god, he's alive," I said. "We need an ambulance here." I like to be helpful by stating the obvious.

"I already called them and should be here any moment," Sparks said tersely.

After several long minutes, one of the officers appeared on the roof, he quickly examined the fragile wooden frame, and he shouted down, "This looks fragile, jury-rigged, if we try to free him, the whole thing could slide off the roof."

"What's the condition of the man?" Sparks shouted up.

"He looks bad, cuts and maybe burns, let me check his pulse." The officer reported.

A loud scream followed by "Shit!" The officer on the roof was holding his hand, shaking it back and forth.

"I touched the wood and it burned me, pretty bad. The wood is coated with some sort of chemical." He called down.

Sparks ordered him off the roof just as the ambulance arrived on scene and the EMTs began to unload their equipment. When the paramedics reached us, she informed them of the situation and told them to treat the burned officer.

If the wood burned the officer after a slight touch, what was it doing to the man tied to the frame? I didn't want to think about it. I hoped the man was unconscious and didn't feel it.

"Suggestions?" Sparks directed this toward Edmund.

"The fire department could be of help here. They have hook and ladder trucks that could reach him." Edmund stated.

Sparks radioed it in. "But what do we do in the meantime, that frame he is on could easily fall off the roof. Edmund, can't you think of something?"

"No, this isn't an area I have had a lot of expertise." He paused for a moment. "Would it be possible to stabilize it with more ropes?" He offered.

"I guess we could try." She sent two officers to retrieve ropes from their cruisers. They hurried around to the back of the building.

By the time the officers carrying the ropes had made it up to the roof, the fire department had arrived. After a quick briefing by Sparks, they sent up a few of their own up to the roof. The fire chief said there was no way they could maneuver their hook and ladder into an useful position, it was just too big and the ground around the observatory was on a slope. The officers on the roof were having a discussion with Sparks and Simmons about what they could tie the ropes to in order to stabilize the frame. By the time the firefighters arrived on the roof, the officers had found a roof vent some distance away and tied one end of each rope to it.

Because of the action playing out on the roof, no one noticed the officer with the burned hand had gotten down from the roof. As he rounded the building, the officer collapsed. Someone yelled "hey" and drew our attention to him, laying on the ground. Sparks and Simmons raced toward him with guns drawn. I hadn't heard any gun shots but I guessed that they wanted to be ready for anything. I instinctively jumped behind a tree for a cover, but Edmund gave me a quizzical look and I returned to his side. After a quick search of the area, Sparks motioned for the EMTs to come over. They expertly retrieved the officer and brought him back to the ambulance.

As they brought him near us, I noticed that the fallen officer was feverish and mumbling. There was no sign of a wound from a gun or knife. The EMTs set to treating his burned hand. Not sure what had caused him to collapse, they discussed among themselves what it could be. Then one of them hit upon the idea that the officer's symptoms were like if he was drugged. Could he have been drugged by touching the wood with his hand? The paramedic felt certain of it. That EMT must have gone to the same school of drawing disparate conclusions as Edmund. I guess it made sense, our killer had made use of poison before.

Sparks relayed that up to the first responders on the roof. "We think the wood is also drugged somehow, so do not touch it with your bare hands. Gloves on, everyone."

They were having difficulty securing the rope to the wood frame. The first board they tied it to simply came off and the whole frame slipped a little down the roof. One of the officers, on instinct, grabbed it. "That chemical is burning through my gloves!" He shouted.

"Let go, let go!" Sparks screamed. He did and it slid a little further toward the edge. "Damn it. I'm going up there."

"Wait a minute, you need to stay here and be in command. Going up there isn't going to help any," Simmons said.

She just gave him a withering look and raced off.

The slow, slow janitor made his way over to us. "That guy isn't supposed to be up there." And I thought I had a talent for stating the obvious.

"Is there a way to access that roof from inside?" Simmons asked the janitor.

"Oh yeah, definitely," the janitor replied nonchalantly. And continued to stare up at the scene on the roof, not offering any more assistance or information.

"Officer Tompkins, go with him and find that entrance, and quickly." The officer put his hand on the janitor's back, firmly guided him back to the front doors.

Watching a life and death situation unfold is not at all like watching a movie. You might be emotionally invested in a movie character and feel grief or apprehension for them. But this was so different. The emotional current of it swept me away. I've never been in a situation like this. I was in a minor car accident in my teens, and remembered having nightmares about that for weeks. This was on a whole new level. Hoping, wishing for a good outcome, but not really thinking it possible. Feeling sorry for the man and wanting him to be rescued and at the same time wondering who he was and how the killer chose him. Does he have a family? What was he doing before he was abducted by the lunatic? And add in all that worry I felt for Sparks and the others that they might get hurt in their attempts to rescue him. I felt a kind of paralysis, not knowing what to do or even feel. To be honest, I wanted to shut my eyes and have all this just go away.

"What's the situation here?" The question brought me out of my self-indulgent musing. I looked over and saw that Captain Burleson was right at our side. Simmons must have jumped a foot and a half when he heard him. After he recovered from the shock, he gave the Captain the run-down of what had happened.

"Simmons, why the hell aren't you up there? Take more initiative," Burleson growled after the officer had finished his synopsis.

"Yes, sir," and with that Simmons began his half-hearted jog around the building.

"Sometimes, I don't know what that officer is thinking. I suppose you were able to figure out some cryptic-ass clues that led you here?" The Captain asked Edmund.

"Yes, sir. We were drinking tea in a..." Edmund started.

"I don't need the details right now. Let's focus on how to get that man down safely," Burleson replied. He stomped off to talk with the fire chief. I forced my attention back to the rescue attempt. It was not going well.

It was nearly impossible to secure the rope without touching the wood, the few times they succeeded to tie off a rope the board they tied it to simply came off. And then the frame slid a little closer to the edge of the roof.

"Edmund, are you sure there is nothing else in the clue to help in this situation?" I asked. "Maybe something from the note."

Edmund pulled it out and reread it.

Dearest Edmund,

I have been watching your love Triangle with interest. I wood have thought that our paths had crossed already, but for now, I'll be hanging out with Paul Stamets and Hugh Culber discussing symbols of the Underworld.

Reed Diamond

Edmund's eyes narrowed for a few seconds then went wide. "What kind of wood is the frame made of?" He shouted up the frazzled first responders.

"How in the hell would I know what kind of wood it is?" Sparks shouted back.

"Is there any writing on the any of the wood?" Edmund replied.

After a frantic search Sparks shouted, "This piece says elm on it. Does that help?"

"Yes, greatly. That will be the stable one. Tie the ropes to that." He yelled to Sparks.

After a bit of a search, she located the right spot on the piece of elm and tied off the ropes. After a few minutes and a few test pulls, it seemed the frame had been stabilized. It was still quite the conundrum to free the man from the structure. Two more officers and one firefighter were treated for chemical burns, but their brief contact with the wood wasn't enough to allow them to be drugged like the first officer.

As they were working to free the man, the Captain turned to Edmund and gruffly said, "All-right, explain how you knew which piece of wood was the right one. But keep it brief, I don't want to be here all night."

Unfazed by the Captain's blatant request, Edmund explained, "He misspelled "would" as "wood," so that led me to realize it was something about one of the pieces of wood, and then his final clue was that they were discussing symbols of the underworld. Two trees were symbols of the underworld: the oak and the elm. Hence, if there was a piece of elm on the scaffolding, it was probably the stable one."

The Captain was shocked, "You just guessed that elm was the right answer?"

"No, I surmised it was. Elm was often used in coffin making; I deduced that our killer would like that fact." Edmund replied with just a touch of defensiveness.

The Captain just shook his head and wandered off.

They carefully lowered the man to the ground. The EMTs surveyed his wounds and were dismayed to realize that every place his body had touched the wood frame was severely burned. They quickly gave him something for the pain he must have been experiencing.

"Will he make it?" Sparks asked the EMTs after climbing down.

"Iffy, at best," replied one of them. "And if he does survive, he'll have a long road of recovery. Whoever did this to him is a monster."

That last phrase stopped me, after all his cutesy clues and riddles, I had started to forget the horrible things that he had done. He was a man who went to extraordinary lengths to torture and kill people for his own delight all the while taunting the police to try to catch him. The word monster did describe him best.

After the EMTs had left with the victim and the police were scouring the grounds for clues, I began to wonder about Edmund and how he was handling this, and, for some reason, how he was handling his new dating life.

"This is some craziness, isn't it?" I said to him.

"Yes," he replied seemingly lost in thought. After a while, he stated, "I should have figured out the importance of the discussing of the underworld clue without your prompting."

"I'm sure you are overwhelmed with the emotion of the night, I know I am," I said encouragingly.

"That seems unlikely," he said with some derision. I guess he doesn't like little things like emotions get in the way of his crime solving genius. Like most people, he doesn't really understand how much his feelings sway him. I didn't point this out, I am sure he would not have received it well.

Once again a comfortable (for him) silence settled on us. But I didn't like it. It's the reporter in me that wants to keep digging for information.

"How do you think Lyman is going to respond to all of this?" I asked with a little bit of anticipatory schadenfreude.

Edmund did his puppy dog head cock and said,"You would think that he would be happy that I am helping to put away a dangerous criminal but he likes to complain about being left out. I tell him what happens, but that just seems to upset him more. He keeps insisting that I solve the clues quicker and has said things like, 'I thought you were supposed to be smart.' I'm not sure dating is for me. It's nice to have company from time to time but he seems to require a lot of emotional upkeep and it is difficult to have someone in my space all the time."

Yes! Edmund, spill that tea! A whole bunch of tea all over the place. And I lapped it up like a dog wearing an ugly Christmas sweater in the desert (this definitely does not count as a sports simile). I knew Lyman was insecure but wow! He was as jealous as a preteen on Instagram. I can't wait to lord it over him. Sometimes, I'm evil, just plain evil. I felt a little justified since he was not supporting Edmund like he should.

"What do you think you'll do about it?" I asked with as much neutrality I could put into my voice.

"I am unsure. What would you recommend?" He replied with genuine innocence.

Dump his sorry ass! Make him grovel! Make him cry!

"I don't think I am the best person to advise you, my track record with relationships isn't the best," I delicately replied.

"How is your relationship with Gustav?" He asked turning the tables on me. I wanted to write that he "asked sweetly," but he didn't ask that way, he asked like an accountant inquiring about your gross adjusted income.

"I can honestly say, great. It is the one of the very best relationships I've been in."

"Not the best?" He inquired.

No, not the best—yet. I haven't told him about you, Sam.

Tuesday August 22, 2017

Dear Sam,

Today was a relatively normal day. No esoteric clues. No hidden messages. No innocent people tortured for a mad man's pleasure. Just nice and normal.

On the good news side, the man who was rescued last night will make a full recovery, a long-but full recovery. Edmund deserves the credit. He is beating this lunatic at his own game. I have hope the police have gathered enough evidence to figure out who this guy is, but there were no fingerprints found on the muffin topper at the coffee shop and there's no hope of any forensic evident from the wood frame having been coated in some kind of chemical. The police are still analyzing what exactly it was. I have an odd feeling this isn't over—not by a long shot.

Tonight, Gustav came over for dinner and we had an uninterrupted evening of food, fun and frivolity. It was exactly what I needed: time alone with this great guy so he could lavish all his attention on me.

He is finishing up the dishes as I write this. Ah, the whole evening was perfect.

I will say good night, Sam, I am going to bed—but hopefully not to sleep.

Thursday August 24, 2017

Dear Sam,

Today started out like a normal day, but that changed quickly. The craziness started with an early text from Sparks asking me to hurry down to the police station.

Here we go again, I thought. I headed down there after kissing my man goodbye (he stayed over every night this week!). On the way, I thought how I hadn't reached out to Edmund this week, but he had not contacted me either. I wonder what had been going on between him and Lyman. I was secretly thrilling to know (and I was pretty sure it was bad news for Lyman). I told myself that I was giving Edmund space to figure out his relationship, but deep down I knew I was being selfish. Edmund needs a friend and his only real option was me. I made a promise to myself to do better in regards to Edmund.

When I got to the police station the conference room was jammed pack with officers and even two agents from the FBI. The tone was much more somber than the last time. Everyone spoke in hushed tones, people congregated in twos and threes, no one was even making wildly inappropriate jokes about things that shouldn't be joked about, but often were. The change in atmosphere might have been chalked up to the presence of the FEDS, but it might have been that the police hadn't cracked this yet despite the abundance of physical evidence. And maybe it was because of the seriousness of the injuries to the man at the museum.

And again, they were all looking at a letter from the killer (his trademark red diamond clearly visible at the bottom of the page.). It read:

My Dearest Edmund,

You have robbed me of my fun twice now, but no more. It is no wonder you have achieved a modicum of success, you've had so much help, standing on the shoulders of giants you must feel so cold. But I don't want you to think I don't like you, I like you very much. We should have a drink together, what do you prefer the old or the new, come, come, tell me. Are you stumped? Doesn't this ring a bell?

Hoping to see you soon,
Tarkshya

A shiver ran through me as I read the killer's closing remark, "hoping to see you soon." I glanced around the room and many of the officers were on their phones googling their little hearts out. But I had a feeling that they weren't going to get lucky this time. I think "our friend" designed this personally for Edmund to figure it.

Edmund stared at the screen, a little more nervous than I have seen him before. I wasn't the only one who noticed this. Detective Simmons was watching him closely with a skeptical look. This wasn't good, I could tell.

"You doing ok?" I quietly ask Edmund.

"No. I can't figure this out at all. It's not like the first time when I knew he hadn't given me enough information. I think all the pieces are there, I just can't fit them together." He said despondently. I think Lyman's steady stream of unencouragement has really eroded Edmund's self confidence. I'm shocked at that, I thought Edmund was undeflatable.

"Is there anything from the clue that you have figured out?" I asked trying to be helpful.

"Ring a bell is an important clue. But how do I figure out which bell? Is it literally a bell, a person named Bell, or even the heroine from Beauty and the Beast." Wow, sarcasm from Edmund, that's new. Or maybe it wasn't sarcasm, maybe he was seriously considering that angle.

"That Belle spells her name with an "e" at the end," I offered in a weak attempt to be helpful.

He stared silently at the letter while officers were leaving to follow up on leads that they had deciphered. After a while, they room was empty, except for Edmund and me.

"Jonathan, what's wrong with me?" His voice cracked with emotion.

That scared me.

"Nothing is wrong with you. Everyone has off days," I said encouragingly.

"Not me. I've always been brilliant, but now..." He sounded like Charlie Gordon from Flowers for Algernon when Charlie realized he was losing his new found intelligence.

"Don't say that. This is a lot of pressure and adding in your new relationship—that's a lot of stress. You can't know how all this would affect you until you go through it. You got this. I know you can do it." I felt awful for him, maybe for the first time in his life he couldn't see the next step forward. He was starting to realize he may not be the smartest person in the room.

I wanted to hug but, you know, it's Edmund and he doesn't like that.

I happened to notice that Simmons was quietly, but forcefully, talking to the Captain in the Captain's office, and they both were glancing in Edmund's direction. Something was definitely up. After Simmons stopped talking, I saw the Captain shake his head no and mouth the some words which looked like "not yet." I felt my stomach drop out like that first hill on The Beast rollercoaster, but I wasn't sure why.

I looked back over to Edmund, but he was gone, he had left the room. I went out to the hallway, but I didn't see him. I texted him, but I got no response. Maybe he did figure out the clue and left but I didn't think so. I can't imagine him leaving without me (oh god, I sound like the stereotypical sidekick). I went out to the parking lot and his car was gone. Without him, I was feeling out of place in the conference room of the police. I decided to join Detective Sparks. She was giving out tasks to various officers.

"Did you see where Edmund went?" I asked when she had finished.

"No, did he leave?" She replied not even looking up from her clipboard.

I nodded.

At that moment, Captain Burleson beckoned me to his office. I exchanged an "Oh Shit" look with Sparks and then dutifully marched into his office. He motioned for me to sit. I sat.

"I don't like the press." He said with all the tact of a lumberjack with a dull axe (is this a sports analogy?). "But I am willing to tolerate your presence because you have always been fair in writing. And because the commissioner is breathing down my neck to have the department be more transparent, so I am giving you access, limited access, to our investigation. You can write about it and I am not allowed to censor what your write, but you can not write until I give your permission. If you cross me and publish without my permission, things in this town will become very difficult for you. Do we have an understanding?"

I gulped and nodded, my voice had left me for a moment. After a long moment I squeaked out, "Yes, sir. I understand."

"Let me spell out what I mean when I say access. You can attend briefings when Edmund is present. You can go to crime scenes when Edmund is present and you can interview officers when Edmund is present. I think you get the idea," The Captain concluded.

"So, I really am Edmund's sidekick," I declared.

The corner's of his mouth turned up for just a second. At that point I knew, I was dismissed. I left his office and looked down at the phone in my hand. It hadn't vibrated or pinged once during my conversation with Burleson. I still hadn't received any reply from Edmund. Glancing about the conference room, I found Sparks and shared my bonus and restriction laid out by the Captain. She smiled wryly.

Next, I told her that Edmund was not answering my texts. I must have had a worried look on my face because she told me that he would be okay. She suggested that I could go back home, then she added, "to Gustav." I excitedly checked my watch and realized he wouldn't be home for a few more hours. I was going to use this unexpected free time to good effect. I decided to make him a special dinner, one from his homeland of Germany, and I chose schnitzel. I made my way over to Dot's Market—the best place in town for great cuts of meat.

The line at the meat counter was unusually long, even for Dot's. The little gentleman in front of me was having trouble deciding what cut of beef he wanted. Every time the butcher showed him the cut he had asked for-by name-he would say no that's not what he meant. I am a patient person…most of the time, well, some of the time. But not when I am trying to get my man's meat. Then I am all eye rolls and heavy sighs. That'll show Mr. Undecided.

During an interminable wait in that uber-slow line at the meat counter, I got a text from Edmund. I breathed a huge sigh of relief—that's the sigh that got Mr. Undecided's attention. He shot me a dirty look. I slightly grimaced-smiled and opened my phone to read Edmund's text. He asked me to meet him at Cox Arboretum asap, I sighed again (did I sigh this much when we were together, Sam?), that was all the way on the other side of town. Ugh, I've been waiting in this line for 20 minutes already and didn't want to lose my spot, I had invested so much time and sighing in this already. I made a big boy decision and decided that this time Gustav wasn't going to lose out to Edmund like so many times before. I texted him back saying I would meet him, but it might be a while. I felt guilty about it, but I firmly decided to finish my shopping and then I would go to meet Edmund. I even stopped to sample a new spicy cheese puff. It was hot, hot, hot! Sam, you remember what spicy foods do to me. All the way to meeting Edmund, I was hiccuping.

Once I got to the Arboretum, I texted him to find out exactly where he was. He responded that he was on the little bridge spanning the turtle pond. With that, I found him easy enough. He was standing in the middle of the bridge resting his chin on his arms which were resting on the railing. I went over to him and stood quietly next to him.

"I come here when I'm troubled, I like to watch the turtles," he said after a while, "Nature has given them a real advantage. They can withdraw from danger into their shells." He paused. "I guess that's something I have been doing my whole life."

My puppy was having a real moment of epiphany. I was surprised and allowed the silence to continue this time, trying to hide my hiccups the best I could.

"Lately, I feel like a turtle on its back—completely helpless and vulnerable. I want to go back to the way it was, before I reached out to you, before this killer started this competition. I was happy and well-protected." He paused here. His next statement was as full of emotion as anything I heard him say up until that point. "I don't want to be responsible for saving people's lives. In that one sentence, he really conveyed the weight he felt on his shoulders. I let him continue. "At first, it was fun and challenging, I really enjoyed matching wits with the killer. But after seeing that man at the museum and how horrible it was that he was tortured; I can't deal with this. I'm going to tell the police that can't help anymore."

I certainly understood how he felt: overwhelmed and powerless. I couldn't blame him for wanting to withdraw, but I knew that the killer would keep terrorizing the city whether Edmund was around or not. And how much more fueled would the killer be if he realized that he beat Edmund and made him run away? I really believed (and do still believe) that Edmund was our best chance to catch this maniac.

"Edmund, I know this is a crappy situation, but we need you." I stifled a hiccup and went on, "Not just the police, it's not just about catching the bad guy, it's about preventing more innocent people from being hurt. We need you, all those people need you. You are literally the only person who can stop our friend."

He remained silent for a long time—even for Edmund. Then he let out a lengthy sigh. (See, I am not the only one).

"You are right. You have been a good friend to me, Jonathan, thank you."

I smiled. "You are wel..." hic "come." I clapped a hand to mouth.

He did his cute puppy head cock and exclaimed, "Say that again."

"You're welcome," I said quizzically.

"No, say it how you said it the first time," he impatiently demanded— good old Edmund is back.

"With the hiccup?"

"Yes," he was exasperated with my lack of comprehension.

"Wel, hic, come?"

A giant lightbulb appeared above his head. "I figured out the clue, let's go." And off he went with me in tow.

As usual, I had no idea what he had figured out. But like a good sidekick, I followed. I drove (I couldn't take another ride with Edmund at the helm). We had pulled out of the parking lot and were driving for a couple minutes before I realized I didn't know where we were going. Edmund had been busy texting Sparks about his discovery.

"Um, Edmund, you haven't let me in on the secret yet," I snarkily told him.

"Oh that. I am thinking of having sex with Lyman," he stated like he was telling me what he had for lunch.

I nearly crashed the car. I certainly was not expecting that. "What? Why? I thought you didn't want to," I managed to get out.

"Well, clearly our relationship isn't working. I am not enjoying his companionship as much and he has been asking me for sex quite a bit. I thought having sex with him might improve things." Edmund is always very clinical, inexperienced, clinical.

"Sex is a complicated thing. And I'm not sure that having sex with him will fix anything. Sex rarely makes a relationship better. And I thought you weren't much of a toucher?" I delicately asked.

"I am not. This is not something I am not eager to do. But I don't want my first relationship to fail because I didn't follow the protocol of being a good boyfriend. A reasonable approach would be to yield to the more experienced partner in the relationship—Lyman. He has told me that this will improve the quality of the relationship. I assume you have had sex with Gustav, did that improve your relationship?"

Oh boy, this is not the conversation to have on your way to prevent a serial killer from torturing another innocent person in a very public place.

"Edmund, that is a very complicated answer and all relationships are different. There is no one approach or formula for success. That's why so many relationships fail. But first, I have a very important question for you. Where are we going?"

"Oh, I guess I didn't tell you. Carillon Park. I was wondering why you went this way, but I thought you knew a short cut." He remarked.

I made a U-turn and headed for the Park. "By the way, how did you figure the clue out?" I was surprised I had to ask. In the past, Edmund was never shy about sharing his genius. But I was eager to move away from the having sex with Lyman conversation.

"The way you said 'welcome' with the pause in the middle reminded me of the letter. Our friend asked if I preferred the old or the new, come, come...that sounded off from the first reading. So, I decided to put the new and come together, Newcome. That's the name of the oldest standing building in the city and then the reference to 'ring a bell', led me to think of the Deed's Carillon. Both of which are in Carillon Park."

"What the hell is a Deed's Carillon?" I asked.

"I thought you went to college? A carillon is a tower with a series of bells that plays music. Deeds is the man it is named after," he explained with just a touch of intellectual snobbery.

"Oh the bell tower. I know that. They decorate it with lights at Christmas time." See, I went to college.

I'm sure he had a comeback to my statement, but thankfully we pulled into the parking lot of the park. The police had just entered right in front of us. I spotted Sparks exiting her car and parked near her. Edmund quickly got her up to speed and then she dispersed her officers, several going to the bell tower, several going to the location of Newcom's Tavern, and the rest began to ask people to leave the park; it was still open for about another hour. Sparks left us to go speak with the administrator of the park.

It wasn't long before one of the officers called us over to the Carillon itself. See, I am expanding my vocabulary. We arrived to see two officers puzzling over a note from "our friend" with his characteristic red diamond at the bottom. It was written in the form of a short poem.

Over sandy dunes
Man soars right into the clouds
He divides himself

From ground to the earth,
Passing a bound'ry in time
He won't recover.

"There's an exhibit on the Wright Brothers here at the park!" I squealed.

"Obviously," Edmund said, but said quietly—so I will count that as a partial victory. "And it is written as haiku."

We raced across the park to the building that housed one of the original Wright Brothers' planes. The officers with us radioed for Sparks to meet us there. She beat us to the exhibit and had an officer keep us out while she and a few others cleared the building. After a few short minutes she walked out, her head hung low.

"Did we get here in time?," I said somberly. I watched the EMTs rush into the building.

"Yes, the Vic will survive, but he is seriously injured." She said quietly.

"Can I go inside and look for another clue?' Edmund asked.

"No, not yet. It isn't a sight for you to see. Our killer tried to cut this man in half...Lengthwise...from his head to his butt. You don't need to see that." She said compassionately.

"And he survived that?" I asked incredulously.

She nodded.

"I think you are being too restrictive. I am sure I can handle the sight of this man. It makes sense that we will find his next clue immediately," Edmund argued.

She was gentle, but absolutely unyielding about this. With many hours or even days before we could see the crime scene, Sparks suggested that we leave and head home. Edmund made her promise to inform him of any clues found. She promised she would.

I gave Edmund a ride back to his car. He was unusually quiet, but I let him be. I wished him good night and eagerly began my ride back home—to Gustav.

Then an unpleasant odor caught my attention. Oh no, the schnitzel!

Friday August 25, 2017

Dear Sam,

I decided not to tell Gustav about the spoiled schnitzel, hoping to surprise him with a homemade dinner sometime soon. As the morning light lit up my apartment, I proudly told him about Edmund asking for relationship advice and me expertly dodging the question.

"Jonathan," he gently chided. "He needs your help. Don't you remember how difficult it was for you when you started dating?"

"But it's just so awkward and just so Lyman King...ugh." He laughed. I smiled. We have fallen into a wonderful routine of dinner, Netflix, bed, then sleep. I could get used to this. He ran off early to his job and I spent the rest of this morning doing a lot of nothing. Just enjoying where I am.

After lunch I got a text from Edmund asking me to pick him up, his car wouldn't start. Sparks had contacted him saying they found a clue at last night's crime scene. I decided to heed Gustav's remonstrations and talk to Edmund about his relationship.

As soon as his seat belt was buckled, I asked him if he talked to Lyman last night.

"No, he wasn't at my apartment and didn't respond to any of my communiques." Edmund replied.

Typical Lyman, he was always such a baby.

"Sometimes people need some alone time," I was playing nice.

Edmund didn't respond.

Once we arrived at the station, Sparks caught us up with the latest.

"We found a note in one of the victim's pockets. He is still in critical condition, but the doctors are hopeful," she said as she laid out a small piece of paper that looked like it was a ticket stub of some sort, "It's written on an admission ticket from Cedar Point."

"Cedar Point? I love their roller coasters! The Millennium Force scares the shit out of me, let's go!" I squealed and clutched Edmond's arm. I got the death stare from both of them. My bad.

On the ticket was written: "Fly north exactly 500 miles."

"500 miles north of where?" I asked.

"I've been thinking about that poem he included in his last message, it's a haiku—it has a structure of 5 syllables in the first line, 7 in the second and 5 in the third. 575–it's the area code for most of New Mexico." Edmund explained.

"Edmund, aren't you jumping to conclusions? Why would you think it has to do with an area code in New Mexico?" I asked unwisely.

"The Cedar Point ticket is referencing not the amusement park, but a city—Cedar Point, New Mexico." He calmly explained.

"What's 500 miles north of Cedar Point, New Mexico?" Sparks asked.

"Nothing that concerns us." Edmund mysteriously replied. "The clue gets us to New Mexico, now we have to found out why."

Edmund was working his magic on his iPhone again. Several long moments passed as Sparks and I just let Edmund do his thing. I was about to go in search of some tea when he finally spoke up,"I've pulled up a list of cities in the 575 area code, let's see which ones make the most sense in context. There's Angel Falls, Sunland Park, Roswell and White Sands. Those are the most obvious ones since they happen to be reminiscent of flight." Edmund stated. "I'll need a map of the U.S. and a ruler."

"What do those have to do with Cedar Point?" I wondered aloud. No one paid me any attention.

We laid it all out on the conference table and measured 500 miles in a roughly northerly direction and nothing really lined up from the first three cities, but when we got to White Sands, Limon, Colorado was exactly 500 miles away.

"Lee-mon, Colorado?" Sparks said.

"It's pronounced Ly-man." Edmund corrected.

The three of us exchanged a look of terror. It wasn't telling us a location, it was telling us a person—Lyman King. Edmund immediately phoned him while Sparks called in some officers and explained the situation; and once she got the address of Lyman's apartment from me, they raced off to find him. Edmund was listening to his phone and put it on speaker for us. There was a new outgoing voicemail message record by Lyman but clearly recorded under duress:

"Edmund, we are like ships that pass in the night. O heart of mine, O Soul that dreads the dark. Is there no hope for me?" The message ended. His voice sounded stressed and confused.

"That's Lyman's voice." His whiny, nasally, irritating voice, but now's not the time to be nibby.

"What was that he said? It sounded like a poem," Sparks noted.

"It sounds like Walt Whitman," I said as I looked it up on my phone, and found it was a line from a William Wadsworth Longfellow poem. "It's from a poem called 'The Theologian's Tale; Elizabeth.' Oh boy, it's a long poem. Digging through this will take a lot of time."

"You are incorrect in your analysis. What's the exact line from the poem?" Edmund asked in his usual demanding tone.

"'Ships that pass in the night, and speak each other in passing, only a signal shown and a distant voice in the darkness.' It's not the same as what Lyman read." I loved pointing out the obvious. Determined to the more helpful, I looked up the whole quote.

"It's not from a Longfellow poem. It's from a Paul Laurence Dunbar poem called 'Ships that Pass in the Night.'"

"The hometown poet," Sparks spoke up.

"Whew, this poem is much shorter. The title doesn't appear in the body of the poem but the other lines do: 'O heart of mine, O soul that dreads the dark! Is there no hope for me?' Could it be this easy? The Paul Laurence Dunbar house?"

"I think that is right, but Lyman won't be there. I suspect there will be another clue to his location." Edmund explained.

I offered to drive us over there (not wanting to experience either Edmund's or Spark's driving style), but Emily overruled me and we piled into her excuse for a car. When we arrived at the home of Paul Laurence Dunbar, now a museum, we saw that good number of people were outside standing around. A couple of officers had gotten there a few minutes ahead of us and emptied the museum.

Apparently this was a field trip for some school, there were gads of kids about and a handful of rather well-built adults. I then notice a van parked near the museum that had writing on the side: Dayton Contemporary Dance Company. The hometown dance company preforms some sort of dance set to some of the poetry of Dunbar for school children. While the police and Edmund ventured inside, I milled about on the lawn—not wanting to be one more person in a tiny house. The fact that there was several muscular men in tight fitting clothing about had nothing to with my decision. I am spoken for…I kept telling myself.

As I was staring into my phone, I felt a tap on my shoulder. I turned round to see a rather handsome dancer looking at me. Well, hello, I thought. He held a business card in his hand. Damn, I had to break it to him that I was already in a committed relationship with someone —kind of two someones and a third someone would only complicate things even more. Before I could tell him so, he spoke.

"Some man give this to me when we first got here, saying if the cops show up give it to the nerdy one."

Ouch. Nerdy, he thinks he I am the nerdy one. This little dancer can shake his money-maker on out of here. Nerdy, indeed.

He continued, "But he went inside before I could. Would you mind giving it to him?" He said with an enchanting smile and a twinkle in his mesmorizing eyes.

Remember Gustav, remember Gustav, remember Gustav! Was my mantra at that moment.

I graciously took the card and thanked him.

I turned to go into the house to show them the clue.

When I found them Edmund stated he was right; Lyman was not at the Paul Laurence Dunbar house. I triumphantly presented the card to Edmund. He was gobsmacked, for once. After Sparks realized what happened she sent me and an officer out to interview the dancer with the mesmorizing eyes. The dancer looked happy to see me again, or my imagination made it so that the dancer looked happy to see me again. The officer asked the man if he could describe who have him the card. He described him as a shabby looking white man who was probably drunk or high. He turned and pointed at a man across the street who was sitting on a bench.

I said goodbye to the dancer with my eyes. The officer and I headed over to the gentleman resting on the bench. The dancer's assessment was dead on: the man was drunk or high. He provided little detail about the person who gave him the card. He couldn't identify his race, his height, his race, his speech, his clothing or anything else. He did proudly display the twenty dollar bill he received from the card giver. The officer was eventually able to get the man to swap out that twenty for a different one. I know the officer was doing his due diligence but I am quite sure that no usable DNA or prints will be found on the bill. We returned back to the Dunbar House.

Edmund and Sparks were discussing the clue on the card, but paused when the officer and I came in. We quickly got them up to speed with what we found out; neither was surprised.

I asked to see the clue, just out of curiousity—not really expecting to contribute much to the unwrapping of the riddle.

"I'm a bit of travel bug, but not Lyman. He is laying in wait for you. But you'll need to go to ground zero.

TFTC"

And of course his trademark red diamond was there. And taped to the note was an old-timey key.

"What do you think that is to?" I asked in reference to the key.

"What does TFTC mean?" Sparks wanted to know.

"Googling," Edmund replied. "It is a song by The Travel Bugs. It's a song about geocaching."

"Geocaching?" Sparks was confused.

Fortunately, I wrote a piece about it nearly five years ago. "It's a hobby where people have planted some small item at a specific location and upload that to the geocaching website and then other people go looking for that item following directions on an app." Look at me! I contributed something useful.

"But where do we start looking?" Sparks asked while Edmund furiously worked his phone.

"Possum Creek Metro Park." Edmund stated after a moment. Both Sparks and I knew enough not to question his reasoning, nor even ask about it. She radioed her officers to go to the Metro Park and we headed their ourselves. On the way, Edmund explained the clue.

"Once I figured out it was a geocaching location, I thought about the key. It's known as a skeleton key, so I searched for that name on the geocaching site and found two locations: one in Ogunquit, Maine or the other in the Possum Creek park. The person who hides the cache names it; for example, Pennyheart or Thingamajig. The killer named this location Skeleton Key."

Sparks radioed out this information to the other officers en route. Unfortunately, the first officers, one being the inept and irritating Detective Simmons, to arrive were not very tech savvy and couldn't figure how to use the geocaching app (or even how to download it). By the time we arrived, they were still in the parking lot arguing over how to get started.

Before the car even stopped, Edmund jumped out and was off, staring at his phone in his hand and walking a straight line. Through a field filled with wild flowers, across a road and into a parking lot and he only stopped when a small lake blocked his direct path. The police and I hurried after him (all except Simmons who said he would stay back and coordinate from the parking lot, apparently he did not heed the Captain's advice of taking more initiative). We caught up to Edmund as he pondered what was the best route to the geocaching location.

Edmund, after a moment's hesitation, chose to go left around the lake. After a couple of hundred feet, he found a narrow strip of land that bridged the the pond. He crossed over and would have plunged straight into some woods if I hadn't stopped him. I told him that it would be best to see if there was trail and pointed to one a little bit to our right.

He hurried to the beaten path and plunged into the woods. It wasn't long before we came across an old, old cemetery—The Kaylor Family cemetery. This cemetery contained graves whose headstones dated back to the early 1800s. Many of the stone markers were weather worn and crumbling. Edmund exclaimed that this is where the

Skeleton Key geocache was. But we soon found something else that was more recent than the old tombstones—a newly dug grave.

"Oh shit, we going to need some shovels," I announced.

We feared the worst. Edmund and I began to dig with our hands and shouted Lyman's name. After a moment, we heard a very muted thumping in response. He was alive!

Sparks radioed the officers to bring shovels, but unfortunately the only shovels the officers had with them were camp shovels and those would make an agonizingly slow job of digging him up. Sparks called in to dispatch and asked for more men, bigger shovels and an ambulance. Edmund took one of the camp shovels and began to methodically (like he would do it any other way) dig around the grave site. Eventually, he started digging a small hole straight down. We all presumed Lyman was in a coffin, but there was no guarantee of that. Knowing this mad man, he could have been just buried in the ground. But the occasionally thumping from the site gave us hope he was inside something.

Sparks and the other officers took turns with the other camp shovel, but the going was indeed slow. Every now and then, we heard that thumping from the ground, even Lyman's thumping sounded whiny and complainy. Shortly before the other officers arrived, Edmund struck something wooden. The other officer digging with him concentrated his efforts to uncover more of the wooden thing. (It's a coffin that we found, I didn't want to leave you in suspense too long).

The EMTs and other officers emerged from the trail and then the unearthing really moved along. Some minutes later Edmund shouted for all the digging to stop. He was listening to what Lyman was shouting to him.

"He's saying be careful," Edmund stated. "Lyman says that the killer put a small box with a scorpion in it into the coffin. If we disturb the coffin, the scorpion will be released."

Well, we tried. Let's call it a night. No, I'm kidding, I would hate for that scorpion to be hurt in his attack on Lyman. Kidding again-ish.

The work proceeded more slowly and carefully now. They had dug up a lot around the head of the coffin. And Edmund was leaning down into the hole and conversing with Lyman. I couldn't hear their conversation but I could tell Edmund was making an effort to be supportive. Try as I might, I just couldn't imagine him saying words of love and support. He might have been just reciting incidents of miraculous survival that he read about, for all I know. The work progressed slowly. Digging up a coffin, even with that many people helping, took a lot longer than I thought it would.

Finally, they were ready to open the coffin and extract Lyman. There was much discussion if it would better to pull the coffin up on to the ground first before opening it or to open it while it was still in the ground. Lyman was pleading with them to be careful, his whining also included wild threats to sue the police department if that scorpion stung him. The police took great care so that the box with the scorpion wouldn't be disturbed. I really give the officers credit, if someone was threatening to sue me while I was saving their ass, I may have not exercised so much caution. They opened the lid to reveal a dirty, sweaty, disheveled Lyman, wearing only his boxers, now that's an image that I can't erase with an entire barrel of mimosas. In between his legs was a small black box. They police wrapped a rope around each leg and an officer grabbed each of his hands. On the count of three, the hoisted him directly out of the coffin and somewhat clumsily dropped him on the ground. An animal control officer had been called in to deal with the scorpion. As soon as Lyman was clear, she jumped down into the hole and gingerly picked up the black box. She felt the box carefully and even shook it a little. She then opened the box and there was a 3 inch red scorpion. She picked it up and bit its head off to the horror of everyone watching.

"Mmm, cinnamon," She said. "It's a gummy."

I laughed and couldn't stop. I walked away from the group into woods surrounding the cemetery, howling. Lyman was scared of a candy scorpion. Oh, he will never live this down, if I have anything to do with it—and I will. When I finally regained my composure, I went back, I saw Lyman being examined by the EMTs. Sparks was interviewing him and Edmund stood off to the side. Some of the police officers were scouring the area for clues.

"I'm glad we found him alive," I said to Edmund.

"Yes, that would have been unfortunate if he had not survived." Edmund said with his usual emotion of blandness.

"I'm sure he'll be ok." I remarked.

"Likely. But I have another worry. What if he comes after you. That would bother me much more than this incident." Edmund said this as if he was worrying about a mosquito bite.

"Edmund, don't say that." I couldn't help but feel a little touched.

He just looked at me. The EMTs began loading Lyman into the ambulance; Edmund walked up and asked Lyman if he would like him to ride in the ambulance with him.

"Hell no! Get away from me. That maniac attacked me, drugged me and buried me in the ground like something out of a freaking Edgar Allan Poe story. All because of you. Stay away! I never want to see you again." Lyman shouted vociferously.

You know, I've always liked Poe.

Saturday September 2, 2017

Dear Sam,
Sparks is throwing a Labor Day BBQ tomorrow and Gustav and I are going. It's been about a week since the Lyman-buried-in-the-ground incident. He still isn't talking to Edmund but I'm not sure it has really affected Edmund at all. He has continued on with his work and whatever it is he does when he is not at work. I, on the other hand, have been very focused on my domestic bliss and, truth be told, these last few days have been pretty awesome—except that there is a serial killer on the lose targeting people in Edmund's life. But it was easier to forget that since my relationship with Gustav is going so well. In relationships, I usually have an irrational fear that the bottom will drop out, but I have always been a glass half-empty and there's a crack in it kind of guy. And I am the one who usually causes the bottom to drop and I myself empty the glass and complain about it afterwards.

And although we have been supes busy with our jobs, those precious few hours at night with him is little something out of a *fairy* tale (pun intended). We really don't do much, watch Netflix, make dinner, chat and laugh, and that other thing...;). I am really ok with this humdrum routine. Look at me being all domesticated!

Sunday September 3, 2017

Dear Sam,

What a great BBQ! It was a great mix of people, food, drinking and relaxing. Edmund came alone, Lyman was keeping true to his tirade and shutting him out of his life. I made sure to spend some extra time with him, just to cheer him up. It is hard to tell if it worked. The only fly on the charcuterie board was when Detective Simmons got up into Edmund's face about the investigation. He implied that Edmund knew more about the killer than he had told and that Edmund was screwing everything up.

"No one, no one could figure out those clues without help. I think you are getting some inside information," Simmons said accusingly.

"That's absurd," I stated in defense of Edmund. "He is not in cahoots with the killer. I've often been with him before one of the killer's crazy schemes is found out by the police. There's no way he could know in advance. You just have to face it, he is that smart." And you're not— is what I wanted to add, but didn't. Mostly because Simmons seems like the type that would have me ticketed by the traffic patrol—just to get even. Or worse.

After his diatribe, he left in a huff.

"Rumor has it, that he is not getting his promotion," Sparks explained. "I mean, he was never Mr. Personality before, but now he is down right mean."

"And a little paranoid," I added.

"And I'm sure his reports are riddled with grammatical errors," Edmund quipped.

Both Sparks and I just looked at him. I think he was trying to be snarky. Maybe I am having a positive influence on him after all.

Friday September 8, 2017

Dear Sam,
So...something new happened tonight. Edmund texted and asked if he could hang out with me and Gustav. I said yes, even though tonight was the night I was finally making schnitzel. I had enough for another person, but Edmond's presence would throw a damp, sweaty, stinky towel on the romance aspect of our dinner. But I hadn't talked or saw my puppy all week. With fall coming on, my freelance work was picking up; and he himself had a lot more to do even though "our friend" had been keeping a low profile.

Gustav worked a little later than normal and arrived home to find Edmund already there sitting on our couch, well, really my couch, but a gay boy can dream. I kinda, sorta, didn't text him about having a guest for dinner. I got caught up in dinner prep and Edmund and I were just chatting up a storm—just like the good old days. What that really means was Edmund was droning on about some obscure bit of trivia and I was nodding.

Gustav was a little surprised to see Edmund in our apartment, but he was a gracious host. I am quite sure that if I walked in on Gustav hanging out with an ex alone in our apartment, you wouldn't use the word gracious to describe me. On a side note, is Edmund an ex? Is there a word for an ex that was never even an ex?

Upon entering Gustav came over a gave me a hello kiss. I was watching Edmund's reaction out of the corner of my eye. It is nearly impossible to detect any emotion on his face, but I think I did see something, something like jealousy perhaps? Or maybe it was just my ego-inflating fantasy.

We did end up having a lovely dinner. It was good conversation, well, Edmund dominated it with lots of trivial trivia and Gustav and I played footsie under the table. He also told us that the police have kept him out of the loop with any new serial killer info. It was clear that Edmund actually missed being around people since Lyman left, so much so that we did have to tell him it was time to go home when the clock passed 9 pm. But as I snuggled into Gustav's arms on the couch while some mindless TV played, I felt good about my friendship with Edmund and my relationship with Gustav. I guess a gay can have it all.

Monday September 11, 2017

Dear Sam,
I woke up this morning to a note taped to my door. It was a copy of Robert Frost's poem, "The Road Not Taken." At first, I thought Gustav put it there as a way of saying good morning. But why would he tape it to my door when he could set in the kitchen or the bathroom? My next guess was a jealous Lyman was trying to warn me away from Edmund, but I dismissed that almost immediately. There was no way Lyman was that literary.

My thoughts went in an even more disturbing direction. This note might be from "our friend." My heart sank. I quickly went back inside and checked on Gustav. Panic surged in me as I saw the empty bed until I heard the flush of a toilet and Gustav emerging from the bathroom with a sleepy grin. I breathed a huge sigh of relief. Then I decided to call Sparks. Apparently she got a note as well, hers simply read "Ettin." She told me that Edmund received one as too, his read, "He clearly was a man of many qualities, even if most of them were bad ones."

We all decided to meet up at the station to figure out these latest riddles. When I went back into the bedroom, Gustav had fallen back asleep. I woke Gustav with a kiss and explained what was happening. He of course volunteered to take the day off, but I said no. I can't let this disrupt his life too. I assured him I would be fine and gathered my accoutrements and headed out to meet up. Sparks and I pulled into the parking lot at the exact same moment and waited outside for Edmund. We were googling what "Ettin" might possibly mean as both of us were commiserating over this whole situation. She was having a great start to her day as well until this. It's a horrible feeling to have someone play life and death games with your life. Throughout this ordeal, I have felt completely helpless (and mostly useless), it's like a hockey player in the penalty box during the Stanley Cup (thank you, Google). After fifteen minutes or so of chatting with Sparks, we realized Edmund hadn't yet arrived. We both texted him immediately. After a couple of seconds we both got a pic, the same pic, in response. It was a image of a billboard with a strange double-headed llama creature and at the bottom was an address: 3211 Needmore Road. (I always thought that that street name was a clever pun).

"How do we know that Edmund sent that pic, and not someone who has Edmund's phone," I said with a quiver in my voice. Sparks dialed Edmund, I could see the sense of dread in her eye.

We were both relieved when Edmund's voice come through. "Detective Sparks, I'm on my way to that address."

"No, you are not. The police will check it out. You stay put." Damn, Sparks got a little scary with her commanding voice. I had no doubt that Edmund, even Edmund, would obey. Good puppy!

She hung up with him and raced inside the station. I followed.

She was already giving orders and officers were scrambling. I had never felt more in the way than at that moment. Sparks, the center of authority, was moving from officer to officer, delegating tasks to each team. She texted Edmund for the location of the billboard and dispatched a squad car there. Then she sent a team of officers to the location Edmund had recited to us. I was a bit in awe of how well she parsed out duties and how unfailingly the officers obeyed. I had my back up against a blank wall near the entrance, trying to look liked I belonged there, but really just trying to stay out of the way. I had just about decided on going home, when she grabbed me by the arm on her way out the door. And off we went.

Sparks decided that we should picked up Edmund at the billboard, and radioed the other officer, giving him a different duty. Arriving at the billboard, Edmund climbed in and we raced to the address on Needmore. It was a small, gray-bricked, warehousey building with two seemingly ordinary doors facing the street and a tiny parking lot. Three other cop cars were already on scene. The delightful detective Simmons, of course, was on scene—he reminds me of that snotty nosed kid in the class that always volunteers before any one else had a chance to. But he, unlike that kid, never really did any real work.

However, he did have the sense to wait for Sparks before entering the building. She parked across the street and gave us explicit orders to stay in the car. She climbed out with her gun drawn and ran over to the huddle of officers. We, of course, got out of the car and stood by the road for a better view.

After a quick conference, two officers, one on each rusty metal door, kicked them open. A large plume of smoke billowed out from each door, the officers scrambled away and Edmund and I ducked behind the car. After a few thunderous heart beats, I looked up again to see nothing more than smoke—no fire, no explosion. Cautiously the officers went into the building. After a moment, an officer exited each door carrying a small trash can with smoke pouring from it. It turned out to be just an ordinary smoke bomb, some how triggered to go off when the door was open.

Sparks told the officers to clear the building, then she and Simmons walked over to us.

"I think I understand the clue I got taped to my door this morning. The poem is about having to make a choice between two options." I explained to the group.

"I looked up what an ettin is. It's a two headed monster." Sparks stated.

"I googled my quote and it's attributed to a science-fiction character named Zaphod Beeblebrox, whoever that is." Edmund lamented.

"Hitchhikers' Guide to the Galaxy," said Sparks and I at the same time. She blushed, I guffawed. Sparks must really be a super sci-fi nerd.

"The character in the book has two heads," I instructed the unenlightened.

"Great book," she said.

"Terrible movie," I replied.

"Can we get back to murderous lunatic?" Edmund chided us, being clearly irritated that we provided more information than he wanted— irony much?

At this point, the officers waved us over after clearing the building. When we got there, each of the officers handed Sparks and Simmons an identical Manila envelope with a small red diamond on the outside.

"This doesn't bode well," I said.

Both of the detectives opened their envelopes and pulled out a single piece of paper.

I was shaking with anticipation on what horribleness was on those papers. On the one Simmons was holding, it read: "1267 N. Keowee street. Good Grief, haven't you figured this out yet?"

On Sparks' paper was written: "Palindromic pastry."

"What do we do now?" I asked the group.

"Clearly, the killer has two victims and we have to choose which one to save," Edmund explained.

"Why can't we save both?" Simmons inquired.

"The idea is that Edmund can't be in two places at once," I put Simmons in his place.

"He's not the only one who can save these people," Simmons retorted with such bitterness that it tasted like burnt coffee.

"All right, everyone calm down. Of course we have to try to save both. Edmund which one do you want to go after?" Sparks asked.

"I'll take the palindromic pastry, that seems more challenging than the other," Edmund stated. Simmons gave him a withering look.

"I'll take the other one," Simmons puffed. "If you agree," he asked permission from Sparks as an afterthought.

"Ok, take a couple of uniforms with you, and keep me updated." Sparks ordered.

He picked two of the other officers and they huddled up trying to figure out the clue. I couldn't help but think that Simmons attempt at leading this would end in disaster. I felt sorry for whoever was waiting to be rescued by team Simmons.

He and his officers quickly left, presumably to go to the address on the paper—well duh, that didn't take a lot of brain power to figure out. I turned back to Edmund and he was busy googling stuff.

"The only pastry shop with even a remotely palindromic name..." He noticed Sparks wasn't, exactly following. "A palindrome is word or phrase that is spelled the same forwards and backwards, like level or race car. Napoleon wrote a famous one, "Able was I ere I saw Ebla..."

"Focus," Sparks reminded him.

"And the only pastry place that would meet that criteria is Ele cake shop. There is a problem, there are two locations," Edmund stated.

"Um...maybe the original one?" I offered.

Sparks was one her phone. "Hi, do you have an order for Reed Diamond. No? I'll try your other location. Thanks." It was my turn to raise a surreptitious eyebrow, when I suddenly remembered that the killer had used the non-de plume of Reed Diamond before. Sparks called the other location and confirmed that there was an order for Reed Diamond there. And off we went.

What was waiting for us at the cake shop was a round 10" birthday cake. It read, "Happy Birthday Krishna" with red and yellow frosting balloons.

Both Sparks and I turned to Edmund, who himself looked mildly puzzled. You could see his head twitch to the left as he tried to decipher this. As he did this for a long time, our anxiety mounted. He set the cake down on one of the small tables in the shop and got out his phone and was furiously searching the internet. After a while, I went over to the little coffee stand in the cake shop and ordered a hot tea latte.

"What? It might be a while before he figures this out," replying to Spark's condemning look.

"When is Krishna's birthday?" Sparks asked.

Edmund replied that it had already passed, it was August 14 for 2017. Each year it landed on a different day based on the full moon calendar. Edmund remarked that it didn't seem to be related to his actual birthday.

"Then what?" I asked wiping a little foam from my lips. Edmund stopped and gave me a strange little look.

"I don't know. It could be referencing the Hindu temple in town, but maybe not. I am certain that I am missing something." I know that figuring this out was literally a matter of life and death, but damn my tea latte was good!

The cake shop owner wandered over to see if everything was all right.

"Yes, a friend of ours made a little scavenger hunt for us and we can't figure out this clue." Sparks explained. She is good at making up lies on the fly!

"I can tell you that your friend had very explicit instructions. I had to make the "a" in "happy," the "t" in "Birthday" and the "r" in Krishna in lettering that was different from the others." She explained. "He did tip very well, so I didn't really mind."

All three of us were stunned that we had overlooked that. To be honest, I wasn't that stunned that I would overlook something like that. But I was stunned that Edmund would. Sparks asked the store owner for a description of the man who placed the order. She replied it was a phone order.

"Atr, tar rat, art, rta, tra are all its anagrams." Edmund stated.

"The RTA is the name of the bus system in town." I cheerfully offered.

"No, there isn't much in common with Krishna and buses. I think it must be art, some Krishna inspired art."

The shop manager was still listening in, then she went over to the community bulletin board that hangs in her store. She plucked a flyer off of it.

"Here, this might help," she said.

The leaflet was advertising a special exhibit at the art museum "Devoted: Visual Performance of Faith." The exhibit had just opened on August 23rd.

Good ole speed dialin' Sparks was already on the phone with the museum.

"In your new exhibit, do you have any art related to Krishna," She asked on speaker phone.
"Yes, a beautiful painting entitled 'The Celebration of the Birth of Krishna.'" The voice replied.

As we were running out to the car, I asked, "Can we eat the cake?"

By the time we arrived at the museum, 6 and a half minutes later, several officers were ushering people out of the museum. A tall, gaunt women was wringing her hands by the main entrance, and I saw one of the officers point Sparks in her direction. She was the curator, Georgine Sand Miner.

"I don't know what you are expecting to find. Your officers came in and just ordered everyone out. Do you think we are employing undocumented workers or smuggling drugs in our artwork." Her vitriol was thick.

"Ma'am, I know this is upsetting, but really it is for everyone's safety. Have you accounted for all your employees? Did they all make it out?"

"Yes, yes, oh wait, I don't remember seeing Jefferson. Jefferson Howard, he is our maintenance man. Let me call him." She pulled a walkie-talkie from her pocket and called out on it. But there was no response.

"Where was he last?" Sparks asked.

"He could be anywhere. He had a lot to do today."

Sparks rushed inside, and we followed, determined not to be left out of it this time. She quickly organized her officers and sent them throughout the building calling out Jefferson's name.

"You two, stay in the foyer. You're lucky I don't make you wait outside," She barked in answer to Edmund's dubious look; and then she was off like a shot.

"I like this place, I've come here from time to time for inspiration," I said in a chit-chatty way to Edmund.

"I've never been here." Edmund replied plainly.

"You should come back and take a look. There are some really great pieces here. It's a surprisingly great collection for a town of our size,"

Edmund didn't reply, instead he just stared at his phone.

As usual my damn ADD was kicking in, so I began to cast about for something to keep my attention. In the center of the building are two courtyards where they hold events, Oktoberfest for one. I meandered out into one and stopped to admire some of the plants and sculptures. I stopped at one gray stone sculpture, it was of a man, sitting in a chair, his face was particularly gruesome. I wondered who would make such an ugly-faced statue and more importantly, why would someone buy it? Something about it, drew my eye back. Oh shit, this wasn't a sculpture, it was a real person painted gray. And he was dead.

I'll admit I panicked just a bit and called out (i.e., screamed like a frightened child) for Sparks and Edmund. I turned away from the horrible scene and tried to keep myself calm. Edmund arrived, he looked at the man and then gently escorted me out of the courtyard as Sparks and two other officers rushed by us to the man. Edmund took me back to the foyer and sat me down on a bench, produce a bottle of water from somewhere. Then he went back to the scene.

It wasn't long before the ambulance arrived, but it seemed an eternity before they wheeled out the gurney with a sheet pulled covering the victim. Damn, we didn't win this one. Edmund came over and sat next to me in silence. For once, I didn't feel the need to fill the air with my superfluous words.

I'm not sure how long we sat in silence, after a while, Sparks came over and filled us in on a few details. Then I noticed that Detective Simmons had arrived. He had a bit of a smug expression.

"Hey, I am sorry that your guy died, but the good news is that we saved one today. He was in an aircraft at the Air Force Museum. The address took us to the site of the old McCook theater, but now that it's torn down, it's just a field. So I thought, McCook Field, which was the original name of the area that now has the Air Force Museum, you know. The line in the note about "Good Grief," that referenced Charlie Brown from the old Peanuts cartoon, so I thought what does that have to do with the Air Force? Then I remembered that Snoopy flew a Sopwith Camel airplane and the museum has one. And our guy was tied up in there." Simmons boasted.

"I'm impressed. You did good work today," Sparks congratulated him. Edmund looked stunned, and I was completely flabbergasted. Could this really be the Detective Simmons that we had come to know and loathe?

"Well, I think I just got lucky," He said with what I interpreted as false humility.

"Luck or no, keep it up," God damn Sparks was always so upbeat.

Simmons strutted out of the museum. Edmund and I waited for Sparks to finish up and drive us back to the station.

It was a quiet drive back, each of us lost in our own thoughts. Sparks dropped off Edmund where he had parked his car near the billboard and then continued on to the station. She chatted a little, but I could tell she was worried about Edmund.

"I think today was tough on him. His first real defeat at the hand of this madman. Try and be extra nice to him," she asked of me. Tough on him? What about me? I'm the one who found the dead man. But I realized I had to put on my grown-up pants and think of Edmund at this time.

"I will. But I think he is tougher than you think. A good night's sleep will do him good." I replied.

"Ugh…how well are you going to sleep tonight?" She asked with a wry, flat smile.

"Not very, I think." I thanked her for the ride and wished her a good evening. I climbed back into my car exhausted and defeated. One thought kept despair at bay—I get to spend the evening with Gustav! I was thinking we could order some Chinese takeout and cuddle on the couch, a perfect, normal evening with my perfect man. Something I felt I desperately needed and was owed. Oh Sam, I know that you have already guessed that it didn't exactly work out the way I thought.

Pulling into the parking lot of my apartment, I immediately spotted Edmund's car. Damn—not tonight. I opened my door to find Gustav and Edmund sitting on the couch. I saw dinner laid out on my tiny dining room table—takeout from the Mexican place that Gustav and I had our first date. It wasn't Chinese food, but it was close enough! I was touched by Gustav's thoughtfulness and aggravated by Edmund's thoughtlessness.

"Edmund, how nice to see you so soon—Hello my Gustav," I greeted my boyfriend with a lingering kiss. Edmund! Take the hint, we want some alone time. But alas, Edmund is not great at reading social cues.

"I wanted to discuss the events of today," he said like a manager going over the agenda for a meeting, "I am not sure I made the right choice." There was just the tiniest little hint of emotion in his voice—regret, guilt, or maybe some frustration. It was slight but it was there.

"I know today was rough. But a little sleep, a little quiet time and you'll have a whole new perspective." I said as cheerfully as I could.

"Yes, sleep often brings clarity of thought." Yes! he's going to leave! "But so does a careful examination and discussion of the relevant material." No! he's going to stay.

"Would you like to stay for dinner, Edmund?" Gustav offered.

"Yes, that would be nice. May I wash my hands?" He asked. We pointed him toward the bathroom. As soon as the door was closed, I turned on Gustav and through clenched teeth I hissed,"What are you doing? We could have had this night to ourselves. You went to the trouble of setting up this romantic dinner. I need to be alone with you."

"Jonathan, we have our whole lives to be alone together. Tonight, your friend needs to be with people. And now that Lyman is out of the picture, he only has us." Gustav grabbed me and held me close, his hands gripping my butt cheeks.   He kissed me deeply, I both loved and loathed him at that moment. Damn it, why does he always take the high road. His hands began massaging my ass and it felt great, then I realized what he was doing.

"You are trying to make me horny, just to torture me. You know I will be going crazy until Edmund leaves—many, many hours from now. You are a little devil," I groused. He laughed, he knew exactly how to press my horny button.

Edmund returned from the bathroom and lectured us on the benefit of bar soap versus liquid soap from a pump. I tried to explain that the liquid soap is aromatic and thematic. I can get a different kind for every holiday and occasion. He looked at me like I just said I bought swamp land in Florida.

We started in on the meal, which I felt was insufficient being divided among three. But I did my best to suffer in silence. Gustav is an excellent conversationalist, he so adroitly drew Edmund out of his shell and kept him from obsessing over the event of the day. On the plus side, I was enthralled at his skill, so much so, that the clock struck 10 before I was realized it.

"Edmund, I am sorry, but you have to go home now. I have an early meeting. But I really did enjoy this evening with you," Gustav said with his usual tact and kindness.

"Yes, I should go. I have a significant amount of work to do, both for the police and several private clients. Thank you for dinner," Edmund gave a strange little look to me and then to Gustav. "Good night." And with that, he departed.

Gustav closed the door, turned the lock and gave me a little look of his own. Then he led me by the hand to the bedroom. Sparks was wrong, I did sleep well that night, just not all that long.

Friday September 15, 2017

Dear Sam,
Every night this week! Every night! Edmund has shown up, uninvited, empty-handed to mooch our food and gobble up our alone time. He is exactly like a puppy, wanting constant attention. On Tuesday and Wednesday nights, Gustav had to work late and so I was left to entertain our guest alone. Do you realize how much reality TV I missed this week? It was a lot! Edmund doesn't like to watch reality TV, he wants to discuss the serial killer or Tibetan weaving techniques or the mating habits of the Fugu fish. ARGH! I don't think I can take much more of it. Fortunately, last night Gustav was home early and helped tremendously in dealing with Edmund. As cold as it is to say this, I have lost all my romantic feelings toward Edmund, I just find him annoying now. As I reread that last sentence, I know it sounds awful, but that's how I feel. On the bright side, Gustav has gone out of his way to show me how much he loves it when I am nice to Edmund. He really brings out the best in me.

But I refuse to let Edmund ruin tonight. It will be me and Gustav and that damn Chinese takeout I've been wanting all week. I am getting some Triple Delight and then something German for dessert. Edmund is not sharing our evening. I'm putting my perfectly pedicured foot down.

Oh by the way, nothing new with the serial killer.

Saturday September 16, 2017

Dear Sam,
I did not share our evening with Edmund—I shared the whole damn night. He somehow invited himself to dinner and then spent the entire night here. He slept on our couch. This is not the Edmund I knew from a couple months ago. Maybe it was the stress of dealing with this serial killer, or maybe it was the stress of having been in a relationship with Lyman—that'll mess anyone up. But he asked, and of course, my Uber-compassionate boyfriend said yes. Next thing I know, he is laying on our couch and telling us about a certain kind of lightbulb that sheds a more natural light than the lightbulbs we currently have.

He woke up and asked us what was for breakfast. Are we running some kind of gay flophouse? A cheery little bed and breakfast with only one unrelenting guest? Edmund was becoming a major block for Gustav and I. Gustav wants to help Edmund in any way, and I just want to help him out the door. I could play the "it's my apartment so it's my way" card but that play would only make me lose out with Gustav. I must sound so selfish. Gustav is the man of my dreams, but that dream keeps having Edmund in it. He is back again tonight and I guess I don't have much choice but to play the gracious host.

And still nothing from the serial killer. He does like to take his time.

Sunday September 17, 2017

Dear Sam,
I have hit upon a wonderful idea for Gustav and I. My snarky comment about running a little gay B&B, got me thinking. A little trip to a nearby bed and breakfast is just the thing to put more zing into our relationship—just to be clear the relationship I am referring to is between me and Gustav—and no one else. I found one in Springboro, not far at all. But it will be perfect for getting away from the stresses in our lives and the inn was a stop on the Underground Railroad--romantic and educational! Unfortunately, they don't have a vacancy until the weekend of September 30th. I guess I can wait a couple of weeks.

Monday September 18, 2017

Dear Sam,
Gustav loved the Bed and Breakfast plan! I haven't been this excited in a long time. Both of our schedules have been crazy busy. There's always an uptick in work for me once school starts. I landed fourteen, that's right fourteen, pieces. All of them have to be submitted by Friday. It's a tall order, but I can do it. If I can keep the distractions at bay. Just as I steeled myself to have a heart to heart about giving Gustav and I some space, Edmund approached me, thanked us for our hospitality and said that he felt it would be best for him to return to his own place. With that, he packed up his things and left. I, of course, told him that he is always welcome here (I was sincere...mostly, well, maybe just minorly). Maybe Gustav was right, he just needed a little time with people to reset himself after the horrible events of the last few weeks. And Gustav and I will have our weekend away to...reset.

I texted a bit with Sparks, but she is holding her cards close to her vest. There is definitely something going on with the serial killer case, I wish she'd trust that I will not publish until I get the ok from Captain Burleson. But I am sure she has her reasons, and the last time a journalist published some unauthorized info, it was a public relations nightmare for the whole department. I'll text Edmund tomorrow about it. He has never kept me out of the loop before, I'm sure I'll get him to spill the beans. If he has any beans to spill.

Wednesday September 20, 2017

Dear Sam,
I've set a goal (how very adult of me!) to start gathering my notes on the serial killer in preparation for writing my award winning, multiple part series on this maniac and how he was caught. My freelance pieces were much easier to finish than I anticipated, leaving me a little free time. The Captain said I couldn't publish until he said so, but he didn't say I couldn't start writing about it. I know you're thinking that I am counting my chickens before they are hatched, but I believe the Captain will keep his word and moreover, I think something big is going on with the case. Maybe an arrest is coming soon. Something most definitely is going on with the case. Sparks has not said a word which says a lot to me. Edmund said he doesn't know any more than I do (and I believe him because if he did know more he would tell me he knows more than I do and he would tell me exactly what more does he know). I must have been asking a little too often, because Sparks is ghosting my calls and texts. I won't bother her much today, but I have a plan. Soon I'll invite her over again for some tapas and Juanita Mores. Heavy on the Juanita Mores.

It seems that the serial killer has "to use the common phrase, done a bunk" — quoting Professor McGonagall is never out of place. There have been no notes, no clues, no signs and most importantly no dead bodies. Edmund told me that one of the traits of a serial killer is a cooling off period between kills. Maybe that's all this is. Or maybe the police are so hot on his trail that he has moved on. Strangely, no one seems concerned about his silence, but I still have a nagging feeling that he's not done yet. But I've always been a worrier.

Friday September 22, 2017

Not only has the serial killer been MIA, but so has Edmund. Don't get me wrong, he hasn't disappeared mysteriously, but something has been occupying his off hours. He wants Gustav and I to meet him tomorrow for brunch at Tanks. A great little bar that serves an amazing breakfast.

Saturday September 23, 2017

Dear Sam,
We met Edmund for brunch and he told us that he has been going on a few dates, but he says he just isn't connecting with any of these guys. I told him to give it time, it might take a while to find someone that is right for him. He, of course, remarked that the matching algorithms in dating apps don't seem to be very accurate. And when I saw "remarked" I really meant lectured.

When we got home from bunch, I immediately jumped onto some gay dating apps and tried to find a good fit for Edmund, the algorithms might not be so accurate, but I am. It was frustrating and thrilling at the same time. Gustav let me indulge my match-making obsession for a couple hours, then pulled an old YouTuber's trick— walking into the room naked. It worked, I was distracted and forgot all about Edmund and his singleness for several wonderful hours. Then he ordered me my favorite Chinese food and we spent the evening enjoying some bad Netflix and just chatting. He is an amazing boyfriend, he knows me so well after such a short time. I am looking forward to this next weekend when we go to the B&B, where it will be just him and I.

Monday September 25, 2017

Dear Sam,
It is over. The hunt for the serial killer is over, the police got him.

My day started with a text from Edmund telling me to get to the police station quick, they received another note from the killer. I raced there and entered into that familiar scene of a gaggle of officers crowding into the conference room and staring at a projection of the killer's letter. Edmund look bleary-eyed and disheveled, he seemed to have reverted back to his pre-Lyman clothing style. I noticed Sparks was off to the side watching the semi-organized chaos, I took a space on the wall next to her.

"What do we know?" I asked as a greeting.

"Not much. This arrived in today's mail. Nothing different from any other communique from this maniac." She said wryly.

"Edmund isn't looking his best," I mentioned.

"Yeah, he has been looking that way since the middle of last week," She replied. "I'm not sure his search for a new boyfriend is a good thing for him."

"Well, he might have fallen into that trap of dating apps. In my youth, I wasted many a late night hour scouring the apps for someone suitable—or even someone just available. In the past, I was not always as discriminating in my dating choices as I am now." I explained.

"You were horny and wanted to hook up—that's not hard to believe," Sparks teased.

Speaking of someone who knows me well only after short time.

In an effort to restore her image of me, I told her of my efforts to explore the world of online dating for Edmund, she gave me an eye roll and a shush. Dang, I really wanted to impress her with my online prowess and matchmaking skills. But I turned my attention to the letter instead.

My dearest Edmund,

How very disappointing. I thought you would be some competition for me. But you are so far behind now, only a nuclear-powered car could catch you up to me. Perhaps like me, you are looking for a mean idea to call your own? But maybe I am being too harsh. You have experienced your first love, which, I am sure, was very distracting. Was it scary? Thunderbolt and lightning, very, very frightening me. Galileo. You have one last chance. Will you best me, I think not.

Tarkshya

I didn't think there was much to this letter, but Edmund was doing his usually googling and unscrambling. I was pretty sure I couldn't be much help to him. Instead, my reporter instinct took over and I observed my surroundings. Detective Simmons was seated right next to the Captain and there was a throng of admiring officers quietly cheering him on—apparently he was trying to solve this as well. He looked calm and cool, like the cat that swallowed the canary. What a change from a few weeks ago when he was the department's whipping boy. Quite the change indeed.

"Simmons seems to have hit his stride," I quietly remarked to Sparks.

"That's an understatement. He can do no wrong now. The Captain has really noticed him and he is back on the fast track to a promotion. I am stunned. With him saving the last vic, he is the favored child. I didn't think the Captain could so easily be swayed," she whispered back.

At that moment, Simmons stood up, looking triumphant and headed out the door with about half a dozen officers. Apparently he didn't want to share his epiphany. I looked over to Edmund, he looked crushed, like a puppy staring out the window as its human leaves for the day without it. Since he wasn't the center of attention, he reverted to what he had been—just Edmund, the math nerd, no longer Edmund the solver of serial killer puzzles. Unlike Simmons, it looked like he got demoted. He sat there a minute or two, then got up and went back to the tiny cubicle that was serving as his office and resumed his non-serial killer work.

My heart broke.

I saw Sparks approach the Captain and ask something; he waved her off without a word. She returned to where I stood, then her radio crackled to life, stating that a 136 was in progress at the Packard Museum on Ludlow.

"A 136?" I quizzed Sparks.

"A hostage situation, weird, do you think that they cornered him?" She mused.

"The serial killer? That would be astounding. Simmons figured this puzzle out and raced there fast enough to catch the killer still at the crime scene? I find that really hard to believe." I said incredulously. I could tell Sparks had the same opinion.

Without Edmund being the chief puzzler solver, we didn't have an excuse to visit the active crime scene. We listened in on the police radio and Sparks interpreted what was going on until the Captain ordered her to go with him to the scene. This was a very anti-climatic ending to this months long drama. Edmund, hearing the drama unfolding on the radio, came over to where I was standing.

Luckily for us, one of the 911 operators who was on her lunch break filled us in on what the radio chatter meant, at least for a few minutes.

"Oh...shots fired," the operator interpreted for us.

"Now they are calling for an ambulance, no, two ambulances. But no code for an officer down, so that's good."

That's about all we got out of her. She went back to her operator job and Edmund slunk back to his cubicle to continue his not-so-exciting work. I was unsure what to do, I was about to leave, having several projects at home that needed attention, when I got a text from Sparks asking to stay until she returned to the station.

About 45 minutes later, she arrived. She caught me up on what happened. They arrived at the Packard Museum after Simmons deciphered the clue, something about a nuclear powered care and thunderbolt, I was only half paying attention since I didn't care that much about how he figured it out. Simmons immediately had the building surrounded and then took two officers into the building, there was some gunfire and Simmons came out saying he saved a victim and shot the serial killer. It turned out that the good detective was also good with his aim, zing! Right between the eyes.

"Something isn't sitting right with me." Confided Sparks. "But I can't talk here and now, how about tapas and cocktails at your place tomorrow night?"

I readily agreed. "What about Edmund? Do you want him with us tomorrow?" I inquired.

She quietly shook her head no.

Tuesday September 26, 2017

Dear Sam,

After a few rounds of eats and drinks, we were ready to get down to business. Spark's fiancé, Daniel M'Cumber, had recently purchased a BMW and Gustav insisted on seeing the car. This might just have been Gustav giving Sparks and I a little time to talk shop.

"Something isn't right with this." Sparks started. "I am not sure we got the right guy. And I am highly suspicious that Simmons cracked this. His performance until very recently had been lackluster and that's being kind."

"Other than Simmons solving this, why do you think that this isn't the right guy?" I probed.

"First of all, we found out his name is Hod Put, he worked for about 20 years at the downtown Rike's until the mid 1980's and since then has been a handyman mostly for a bunch of different apartment complexes and businesses."

"Rikes? The department store? Didn't they go out of business like 30 years ago? The only thing I remember about it was my aunts telling me about their wonderful Christmas displays that they put up in their store windows."

"Yep. We searched his apartment, a small one-bedroom just across the river. He didn't have a computer or printer or even a TV. No collection of books, no bromide, nothing that ties him to the other murders. The envelopes in his apartment do not match the ones the serial killer mailed. He did graduate from Chaminade High School in 1963. Maybe he remembered a lot of chemistry from then." She commented wryly.

"How old is this guy?" I asked in astonishment.

"72." She replied.

"How could a 72 year old rig up that scaffolding on the museum? How could he cut that man in half at the Wright Brother's exhibit? How could he do any of the bat shit crazy things that he did?" I asked incredulous.

"I agree," Sparks said. "I think we both know that this guy is not our serial killer. That leaves us two possibilities. The serial killer set this guy up to take the blame, or Simmons faked this to make himself look better."

"Whoa. That would be really stupid of Simmons. He would have to know that he would be found out and pretty quickly."

"I agree again. But he has done some pretty stupid shit in the past. A more disturbing thought is that if he did set this all up, he murdered that old man just to further his career."

That froze me in my tracks. Could he really be that evil?

"Have you spoken to the Captain about this?"

"Not yet, he is pretty euphoric over solving this one. He has scheduled a news conference for tomorrow afternoon. I guess I'll speak to him in the morning and hope he listens to reason."

"What has Simmons said about this?"

"I haven't spoken with him. As an officer involved in a shooting, he is automatically put on paid administrative leave. Though I think the Captain is planning on bringing him in for the news conference. The thought of his smug, smiling face on the news is nauseating."

"Why didn't you want Edmund here? I kind of feel like he deserves to know this." I put forth.

"I think he does too, but there's something else weird going on. The Captain, at Simmons urging, has told us to limit the information that goes to Edmund. That's all he would say. When I asked for more details, I was told that he had his reasons and I was summarily dismissed from his office. And by extension, I am supposed to be limiting the information that comes your way," she explained.

"Oh, I just realized that this also means that our serial killer is still out there," I ruefully lamented. I also realized that maybe the department is looking at Edmund as more of suspect, of having some involvement in this. That really brought my mood down.

"No need to remind me," and with that our evening ended dismally.

Wednesday September 27, 2017

Dear Sam,

This morning, a text from Sparks woke me up and kept me awake. The man shot by Simmons was definitely not the serial killer. She adroitly summed up the evidence that showed Hod Put was not the murderer, which meant that the real killer is still out there. I asked about Simmons and what will happen to him and she replied she honestly didn't know.

Mercifully, I have a lot to do this week and that helped me to keep my mind off things. I have seven more freelance pieces to finish up by Friday before Gustav and I leave for the weekend away. We both have talked about how much we are looking forward to this, but I think we both were holding our breath to see if it really happens. What did Scottish poet Robert Burns say? "The best laid schemes o' Mice an' Men Gang aft agley." Or in non-Scottish dialect, the best laid plans of Mice and Men often go astray. Damn, I need this weekend, so I am hoping the killer lays low for a few more days.

I haven't heard from Edmund since Monday. My texts and calls have gone unanswered. I can't tell if this is a good sign or bad. Did he find a guy to hang with? Is he depressed at the lack of good men out there (we've all been there!)? I texted Sparks and she said he has been showing up to work but he has been uncharacteristically quiet. I asked what his mood was, she replied with the shrugging-shoulders emoji.

Friday September 29, 2017

Dear Sam,

Today, Edmund was brought into the station for questioning about the serial killer's murders. Spark's text made it sound like they were accusing him of at least some of the murders. We all know that's absurd, I was with him during at least one of the murder's time frame, if not several. Sparks explained to me that one of the suspicious behaviors that the police take note of is when someone inserts themselves into an investigation. Apparently, criminals do this often enough that the police are watching for it. And Edmund certainly did insert himself into this investigation; as you know, he pretty much got the investigation started. I am sure once they talk to Edmund, he will explain himself and all this suspicion will go away. The police will realize their mistake and let him go. The police, after all, are reasonable people. That's what I thought until I got a knock at my door.

Two uniformed officers said that they would like me to go with them down to the station for questioning. About what I asked. They said there are somethings they would like me to clear up. I started to protest, but realized it was futile. When I asked how long it would take, they said not long. I had a strong suspicion that this would take a lot longer than "not long." The one thought continually running through my head was about our plans for the weekend. I could only hope that they let me go in time so that those plans wouldn't be ruined.

Once we arrived at the station, I was put into a very small interview room with nothing more than a small table (bolted to the floor) and two chairs. And I waited, and waited, and waited. I texted Gustav to let him know what was going on. He was concerned, really concerned, to the point that he alarmed me. He kept urging me to contact a lawyer. He said in preparation for his trip to America, his company spent a whole day training him how to deal with the US police and courts, in case it was necessary. I told him he was overreacting. I'm sure the police wanted to clear up a few things and I said I was more concerned about Edmund than myself. In the middle of this text conversation, in walked Detective Simmons with another officer. The frumpy detective sat in the other chair; the other officer stood stoicly by the door.

"I thought you were on administrative leave after the shooting the other day?" I asked.

"The inner workings of the police are not your business. Let's talk about your collaboration with Edmund Pollard." He said rather brusquely.

I picked my phone up off the table to text Sparks to tell her what the hell was going on when he grabbed it out of my hand.

"I need your full attention." He sneered as he powered down my phone. A little part of my soul powered down with it.

"I'm pretty sure you can't take my property without my permission or a warrant, and I don't even need to be here, unless you are arresting me. Are you?"

"I'll decide that after we talk," He replied. "So, start talking."

"Generally, in an interview, the interviewer, YOU, asks questions to the interviewee, ME." I whipped out my best passive aggressive tone.

"We know that Pollard is responsible for the murders." He screamed at me.

"That is not a question." I quietly replied.

"Tell us how he did it," Simmons yelled.

"Still not a question," I intoned.

"You think you are pretty cute, don't ya?" He really was doing a good job of setting me for great responses. Of course I do think I am pretty cute. I was in full snark mode.

"That is a question, but fairly immaterial. If you have specific times and dates that you would like me to corroborate Edmund's alibis I would be happy to do so. If you are just going to scream at me, then I think this interview is over." I said calmly.

"I know you would lie for him, so I'm not going to waste my time asking you for those," he snidely replied.

"Then why am I here? I could be home packing," I said with a hint of exasperation.

"Fleeing the jurisdiction?" Simmons snidely asked.

"No, I'm taking my boyfriend to a little B&B in Springboro for the weekend, if you have to know," I explained.

"Your boyfriend." He flipped open his little notebook. "That would be Gustav Richter. An illegal from Germany—home of the nazis." He replied contemptuously.

"He's not an illegal. He is here on a valid work visa." I defended.

"I'm going to check into that. Now that's talk about Pollard's aberrant behavior."

Over the next four hours, he tried to manipulate me into proving Edmund was guilty. He brought up Edmund's idiosyncrasies, but from what I could tell he didn't have any real evidence. He made me go over and over the details of each of the murders and how Edmund solved them. All the while, degrading Edmund every chance he got. But after it all, he said I could go and he gave back my iPhone. I turned it on and saw that I had several messages from Sparks, a ton of texts from Gustav and six missed calls from him. I texted Sparks back to ask how Simmons could have returned to work so soon, and as I was walking out through the lobby, Gustav was there waiting from me. He gave me the biggest hug and asked if I was all right. I think it was at this moment that I realized that this is the man I want to spend the rest of my life with. After all the worry, the craziness, the mortal danger he had gone through because of me, he didn't run away. And I haven't pushed him away. He is a keeper. There is a Harry Potter reference just waiting to be used here, but for the sake of brevity, I will forgo. I said I was fine and told him I would share all the details when we were on our way to the Bed and Breakfast.

Gustav got into his car and followed me back to my place. On the drive back, I realized Edmund had not texted me. I wondered how his interview went. As soon as I pulled into my apartment complex's parking lot, I called him. It went right to voicemail. That's not a good sign. I texted Sparks to ask about him. She replied back that he was still being interviewed. Oh, shit, guilt started wracking my innards. I should stick around this weekend to help him, right? But I cannot cancel my plans with Gustav. What's a boy to do?

I asked Sparks. She said go. She'll look after Edmund this weekend. Her fiancé was out of town at a solar power convention—boring! Her word, not mine. I was thinking it, but she actually said it.

I felt relieved, not in Sparks calling the convention boring, but that she will look after Edmund. Gustav had arrived by this time and we threw some things together and headed out for our romantic getaway. He wanted to drive his new car, well, newish car—he had recently purchased a 2005 Pontiac Sunfire. He thought it was a muscle car, I let him believe that. And I was perfectly fine with his driving, he is used to driving 120 miles an hour on the Autobahn. On the drive down, he told me that he had called ahead and explained that we were running late. We missed dinner there, but the receptionist recommended a great little take-out place. We followed her suggestion and got some rather good provender. We did a quick checkin to the in and was quickly escorted to our luxurious room. The food was great, even more so in this beautiful environment. We retired to the bed early—the week had been exhausting, but we both had energy enough for a little dessert. This weekend is going to be unforgettable.

Saturday September 30, 2017

Dear Sam,

The Bed and Breakfast is absolutely charming. Very well furnished, comfortable and cozy and serene. The breakfast this morning was full of home-made awesomeness; we dined with a nice Canadian couple traveling the US. We talked and laughed with them until it was almost lunch time. They graciously invited us out to lunch and we accepted, they had researched a local pub—it wasn't anything fancy, but it was tasty. After lunch, we all went on a tour of the B&B and its property. The owner explained how it was used as a stop on the Underground Railroad. The Canadians, Mr. & Mrs. Kessler, (his name was Bert, I honestly don't remember her name) then invited us to dine at their table for dinner at the B&B. We thought this was incredibly gracious of them, until we realized that we were the only other people staying at the Inn. So it was a foregone conclusion that we would be dining with them.

At 7:30, we entered the dining room and were awed by its elegance. A monolithic chandelier hung over the centuries old oak table. It was polished to a high shine. Their were more than a dozen utensils at each place setting, I felt a bit awkward, not knowing when to use which utensil. I hoped I could watch the others and use the right implement at the right time. Being afflicted (or perhaps gifted) with ADD, the artwork on the walls caught my attention next and I wandered off to take a closer look. After several long minutes, Gustav had to call me back, like a wayward puppy, and gently chided me that it would rude to ignore our dinner companions.

The food matched the setting in its elegance. Whereas breakfast was rustic and comfortable, dinner in contrast, was sophisticated and epicurean. Seven courses were served and at each the server would explain what it consisted of, how it was prepared, it's history as a local cuisine item and which utensil to use. It was my personal version of Dinner Etiquette for Dummies. I could spend several hours describing each dish, its appearance and aroma, its texture and flavor, but brief let me be. I did take a ton of pics on my phone to make my online entourage jealous. (Side note: Gustav and I both agreed no social media for the whole weekend, it was tough, but I kept that promise). Brevity notwithstanding, it would be a dishonor to the chef to not to describe the dessert. It was a take on tiramisu, the coffee smell and flavor were so deliciously strong but not overpowering, the creaminess and sensuousness of the filling and chocolate were perfect. This is the stuff of a foodie's wet dream.

Fully stuffed and immensely contented, we parted company with our Canadian friends, and Gustav and I went up to our room. We settled in, turned off the lights and lit some candles. Then we sprawled out on the bed, shedding some unnecessary clothing. We were canoodling and chatting about nothing when a text come through from Sparks, it was brief (God bless Sparks!): "Edmund is fine, we are hanging."

I felt much better after that. Gustav found something soft and romantic to play on his phone. I snuggled close to him on the spacious king sized bed and he leaned over and kissed me sweetly and fervently. His lips always felt so soft, but firm—everything about how is muscles. He kissed me with a gentle fierceness. I unbuttoned his dress shirt and ran my hand over that Teutonic chest. So very sculpted and firm. I could be content with just playing with his chest all night long. But that was not his plan. He pulled my polo off and pinned my arms above my head. His tongue began to ravage my arms, especially my pits, first one then the other. He knows that drives me wild, as do you, Sam. I let him do so as long as he liked, squirming on the bed all the while. He then undid the button on my skinny jeans and slid them off. I didn't even care that he just threw them on the floor instead of hanging them up. He stopped to admire my new Andrew Christians I had bought just for this occasion. He looked at them, then up at my face and then back to them again. Weirdly, it reminded of Edmund's reaction to seeing me in my briefs back at the Purkapile farm. I quickly dismissed that memory and went in for his pants. I fumbled a bit with his belt buckle, it was a new one that was a ratchet belt, but got it undone soon enough. He just smiled at my attempt, savoring the anticipation of what was to come. I unfastened his pants and slid them down and off. It was my turn to stare at him. Such a man, my man. His legs wonderfully strong, his chest beautifully muscled and the parts in between gave me no cause for complaint. I slid my hand into his boxers and that's when we heard the scream.

We jumped out of bed and ran to the door, opening it wide. The screaming continued and it clearly was coming from the Canadians' bedroom. A second before we knocked, the door was flung wide open and Mrs. Kessler screamed and bolted down the stairs crying, "Call the police!" We looked into the room and saw Mr. Kessler leaning out the window, he was at an odd angle. We went to him and pulled him back in and laid him on the bed, he was unconscious.

Gustav pointed to a syringe that was sticking out of his side, only half-depressed—some sort of liquid was clearly still in the tube. An uncontrollable shiver ran through my body that had nothing to do with the fact I was only wearing my canary yellow Andrew Christian briefs. I realized that both Gustav and I were both in our underwear.

A moment later, Mrs. Kessler and the B&B owner hurried into the room asking what had happened. "Mrs. Kessler said that someone had tried to climb in through the window," the innkeeper said puzzled.

We explained that we responded to her screams and found Mr. Kessler hanging out the window with a syringe in his side. "What the hell," she stammered in disbelief. "Who? What? Why would someone inject him and with what?"

"I think I know what's in the syringe and who it might have injected him," I announced quietly.
Gustav's eyes went wide with fear. And he just shook his head, dismayed.

"It's Rocuronium bromide, it is a form of curare. It just knocked him out, he should recover in a little while." I said in an attempt to be comforting. " It's a long story about who did this. I think we should wait for..."

At that moment, all the lights went out, I watched the ceiling fan slow its spinning blades until it died. Then we all just looked at each other not moving, after a few seconds, as if a spell released us, both Gustav and I rushed to shut the door and began to drag a heavy armoire in front of it to serve as a barricade.

"Is that really necessary?" The owner asked. "You are scratching the floor. That's the original wood. It had cost a fortune to refinish."

It took all I had to bite back the snarkiest reply I had ever thought of.

Instead I said, "The man we are dealing with is incredibly dangerous. He has already killed at least half a dozen people, probably more. It is the serial killer you might have read about in the newspapers terrorizing Dayton."

The owner clasped a hand over her mouth in shock. Mrs. Kessler's knees gave out and sank to the floor. Gustav, who had been busy shutting and locking the windows, had returned just in time to catch her.

Don't ask me how I had my cell phone in my hand; I must have subconsciously grabbed it after we heard Mrs. Kessler scream. I was on it in an instant calling Sparks

"He's here at the Bed and Breakfast!" I loudly whispered into the phone.

"Who?" Who the hell do you think it is? Seriously, Sparks work with me here.

"The killer, he is here. He tried to attack another guest. And now the power has been cut and we are holed up in a bedroom." I explained trying to keep the panic out of my voice.

"You are in Springboro, right? I'm calling their PD. Don't leave the bedroom and, Jonathan, don't die," I had to roll my eyes at that cliche. My life is hanging by a thread and she goes for the cheesiest line ever. Oh Sparks.

I put my phone down on the armoire and went to the door and listened. Not a sound. Several long thunderous heart beats later, I heard heavy foots mounting the stairs. Then a severe knocking on the door that scared the shit out of us.

"Springboro police, it's ok, you can come out," said a muffled voice

Maybe after months of facing off against a serial killer had made me paranoid. "Don't open that door," I told the others. "How can we be sure?"

The others looked at me with that you can't be serious look. But their looks also clearly said if you don't believe it is the police then do something about it. So, I did.

"Um, not that I am doubting you, but how do we know you are really the police?" I replied to whoever was beyond that door.

"Who else would come to your rescue?" The voice said incredulously.

"If this was a horror movie, you would be the killer," I retorted.

"But it's not," the voice replied in a sickly sweet tone. "So, just open the door and this will all be over."

Another cold chill swept through my body. At that moment, a moan escaped from Mr. Kessler and we all left the door and went across the room to the bed to see if he was coming around. Then, out of nowhere, four shots sounded, and we saw four small holes in the door. And we saw the holes in the opposite wall. Gustav on instinct threw himself against the armoire, crouching low, as the door shuddered from the blow coming from the other side. He pushed it in front of the bedroom door as the innkeeper shrieked something about scratching the teak hardwood floors. I saw that the door gave a little as the unknown was trying to still kick the door in. I rushed over to throw my weight in to help. Normally, my weight isn't that significant, but I did just come from a 12 pound dinner! Gustav and I managed to push the door completely closed again. I swore I heard a hushed, moaned string of explitives from the other side of the door.

A few moments of agonized silence went by. And then a few more and a few more. In the distance, we heard a siren. I was unsure if it was even related to our situation, but nonetheless, it brought me hope. A few more minutes, brought the sound of many feet ascending the stairs and a rapping on the bedroom door. I'm holding on to my belief that police everywhere are trained to knock in the exact same way. "Springboro Police, come out with your hands up." We heard a voice say.

"Not to be difficult, but how do we know it is really the police and not the killer trying to get us to open the door?" I shouted.

"I can assure that we are really the police," the voice insisted. I was not assured. I called Sparks, who was driving down to us, and asked how I could verify if it's the real police. She suggested I ask the officer's name. I did. He replied with a name, but that didn't help. I explained that I was friends with Detective Emily Sparks of the Dayton PD and she would be here momentarily and then we would open the door. That was not received well. The officer threatened us with obstruction of justice if we didn't follow his directives. We still waited. But it was much longer before we heard Spark's voice shouting up from the bottom of the stairs telling us it was safe to open the door. We did.

The police rushed in with weapons drawn, commanding us to lie down on the floor. We complied and were thoroughly searched. Not that Gustav and I had much clothing on to hide anything. I heard

Sparks explaining to the detective in charge who we were and that we should not be detained at the station. We each gave our separate statement to an officer. By this time, Mr. Kessler was conscious and talking.

After what seemed like hours upon hours, we were free to go. The innkeeper promised to refund our money and give us a free weekend —which I though was incredibly generous because I held her blameless in this—and we did put some seriously wicked scratches in her one-hundred and seventy year old floor. Truth be told, if anyone is to blame, it would be us. The innkeeper and the Kesslers would not have been in this horrible situation if we hadn't selfishly wanted to go on this little vacation. After all, we know that the killer might come after us. We think the reason he tried to break into the Kessler's room was he mistook it for ours. We had turned off all the lights and were just using candles, but they still had their lights on.

As we descended the stairs, we saw Edmund standing near Sparks with his usual emotionless expression.

"Edmund, you came down to see us that we were safe," I said touched with his caring.

"Sparks just told me to come along. Did you see the killer?" He asked with a tad of eagerness in his voice.

"No, the other couple staying here did, but they couldn't give much of a description. Just someone in dark clothing."

Edmund seemed disappointed. He tried to look around and do a little investigating of his own, but the Springboro PD were having none of it.

As we walked back to our cars, Sparks brought up an interesting thought.

"Strange as it sounds, this might be a good sign. He was not nearly as cautious as he had been before—he might be feeling desperate and that could make him reckless. And that's when he will make a mistake." Yeah, a mistake that nearly cost us our lives. Some cold comfort it would be for me to be dead, but the killer apprehended. She then said, "Damn, Jonathan, who knew Gustav had such a hot bod?" That got me to smile, for a moment, then I snarked, "What about my hot bod?"

We dejectedly headed home, but we didn't feel safe there. We debated for a while on where we could stay. Gustav wanted to ask Mama Wertman, but I was dead set against it. I refused to put anyone else at risk. But Gustav, in his usual clear-mindedness, pointed out that it would be nearly impossible for the killer to figure out that we would be staying at her house. He also pointed out that she owns a bakery and is a fantastic cook. Who could say no to such good foodie logic?

Sunday October 1, 2017

Dear Sam,
Mama, as she insisted I call her, gave us the royal treatment: A huge German breakfast with fresh baked bread and some hard-to-pronounce cheeses and some tasty sausages. All during breakfast, she not so subtly hinted that we are perfect for each other and that she would be happy to make us all the bread we would need for our wedding reception. This was a little awkward, but I am not going to lie, as you know, I have recently been thinking that a permanent thing with Gustav would make me very happy.

Next, she brought out a German newspaper from about a week ago. Mama pointed to the headline and Gustav spilt his coffee grabbing the paper. He read with a feverish appetite.

"I don't believe it! I know that this was happening at some point, but I didn't know it would be so soon!' He exclaimed.

Mama and Gustav conversed in a fast paced dialogue in German, but then he turned to me and said, "Where are my manners?! This article is saying that gay marriage is now legal in Germany starting today, this very day."

I was stunned that America got marriage equality before Germany and even more stunned that today was the date it started—just when Mama was hinting about us getting married.

"But Mama, you know it is too soon, we have only known each other for a few months," Gustav explained.

"What does that matter? When I laid eyes on my Augustus for the first time, I knew I would marry him. And when I kissed him for the first time—not one drop of doubt remained." She replied. "I know that you feel the same about Jonathan, for the way you talk to me about him."

"Oh, you have talked to Mama about me?" I kidded Gustav while arching my eyebrow.

"I have no shame in saying, I have. It is hard not to share the good things that happen in your life with the people that matter most," Gustav said in his usual cheery tone. "And to be completely honest, this relationship we have is more complicated than most I have been in. Serial killers, police chases, and an enigmatic rival for your attention. So, I need an objective perspective from time to time."

I blushed a little at that for a whole host of reasons.

"Life is always uncertain," Mama told us, "Sometimes it is better to act than overthink. If I had waited with my Augustus, we would have had less time together, even less than we did." A tinge of sadness entered her voice.

Gustav stood up and hugged her, but looked at me with a strange glint in his eye. I think he is taking her words to heart. Sam, I never thought I would get over you, but I think Gustav has shown me that one love lost doesn't mean all love is lost. I think I can still love you from my past, and love him in my present. I swear to God, I am a professional writer even though I produce overly sentimental dribble like this.

Friday October 6, 2017

Dear Sam,

It has been a quiet week. There has been no sign of the serial killer, no notes, no threats, no attacks. Maybe the close call at the Bed and Breakfast scared him away. I don't really believe that, but I guess it's possible. I've reached out to Edmund many times this week, but he is ghosting me for some reason. I even stopped by the police station yesterday, but somehow he knew I was coming and ducked out before I could talk to him. Gustav is encouraging me to keep trying, but I am ready to cut him loose and move on. I know Edmund needs me more than I need him, so I don't want to be selfish, but I can only try so much. He has to want to continue our friendship, too.

On the brighter side, you know this is my favorite time of year with fall settling in and Halloween coming up. I've been taking long walks in the evening, sometimes Gustav comes with, sometimes not. How can I be this happy with a mad man trying to kill me and terrorizing the city? It is such a paradox. But I am really trying to put this serial killer experience behind me and move on. To tell the truth, I don't think this serial killer business is ready for me to be behind it. I have begun writing some about it. Trying to put these events into words is a doubled edged sword (a fencing metaphor?), it is healing some, but it also reminds me that it is still unresolved.

Monday October 9, 2017

Dear Sam,

I knew it was too good to last. Edmund got another letter from the serial killer today. It was his usual cryptic crap. Sparks let me know early this afternoon and invited me down to the station to lend a hand. I was surprised that the Captain allowed this, Sparks said that nothing really came of my interview or Edmund's. I was happy to go. I wanted to be there to be supportive of Edmund. I hadn't seen him in almost two weeks. He looked pale and sickly and sad, forlorn really. I sidled up to him as he was pondering the pontiff privately (is this alliteration too much?). I asked him how he was doing and he gave the universal answer for "leave me alone," he said "fine."

I tried to engage him more in conversation but he didn't want to. So, I stood by and watched, like any good sidekick would. Sparks came over and chatted with me about the usual chit chat, her fiancé landed a big solar contract, I told her my boyfriend was in Chicago for the week. Sparks knows me well and is really good at putting me ease, I was going to say as much to her when the Captain put the latest letter on the projector.

The letter read:

Dear Edmund,

I cannot tell you how much I have enjoyed seeing you fail time after time. I almost feel like making this easy on you and give you something simple this time. But I do have a reputation to maintain, and even though I am king of all I see, I would trade my kingdom for a voice. Nevertheless, let's see how you do with this:

Hammurabi
De Molay
VIXI

Msiniymithilpi
Lupine
Solar Noon

Gershom

Your Best Friend,
Tarkshya

I couldn't make heads or tails from it. But Edmund was working hard. I was eyeing Simmons from across the room; he was just chatting it up with his cop cronies. He wasn't even pretending to work on this puzzle. It was like he didn't care anymore, maybe he thought he had impressed the Captain enough so that he could relax.

"Too easy," Edmund muttered. Not in a boast, but almost in disbelief. Sparks and I went over to see what he meant.

"This puzzle is way simpler than anything he has given us before," Edmund stated.

"Explain it to us yokels, please." Sparks requested.

"Hammurabi and De Molay both have to do with Friday the 13th, this Friday. The VIXI in Latin roughly translates to "I have lived" which implies death, and it is an anagram of XVII which is 17 in Roman numerals, which is Italy's unlucky number, another reference to Friday the 13th. The msiniymithilpi is the Shawnee name for the Great Miami river, which is the river that runs through downtown, and Lupine is Latin for wolf. Solar noon refers to the time that the sun is at its zenith. So, he is telling us that at this location, the intersection of the Great Miami River and Wolf Creek, on Friday 13th at 1:22 pm that someone is going to die. He tells us where, he tells us when, but the only clue to who is the name Gershom. Gershom is the name Moses gave to his first-born son in the second chapter of Exodus. They are a few other brief mentions of that name throughout the Old Testament, but even with all that I am unsure who he is next victim will be."

"Then we got the bastard," voice snarled behind me. I turned to see Simmons eavesdropping on us. "We will flood the area with police and he won't get away this time, the bastard."

Eavesdropping of course is a terrible social faux pas, but using the word "bastard" twice in one sentence is almost unforgivable. The English language is replete with wonderful words to describe a heinous person, and he used the same one twice, what a troglodyte.

Simmons grabbed Edmund's arm and pulled him to the Captain. The frumpy detective barked an order to Edmund to explain his findings to the him. Which Edmund did. As he finished, Simmons jumped in and explained to the Captain how they could capture the killer by laying out a dragnet of officers in the area. The Captain listened and then began to give orders to prepare for Friday's operation. Simmons looked like the cat that swallowed the canary. I did notice that Edmund tried to tell the Captain something, but was brushed off. He returned to us dejected.

"It's too easy. I have a feeling that the killer is tricking us somehow." Edmund relayed, then added, "But on the other hand, maybe I am overthinking this." Gone was his confidence, his unwavering belief that he knew what was right, more than anyone else; this thing had beaten him and I had a feeling that the killer knew that and relished it.

"You are not overthinking this," Sparks jumped in, "Your instincts are good, I'll speak to the Captain and get him to listen to you."

She was interrupted by Simmons calling for attention from the room. "I want to make this clear, we only shoot to protect a vic, and no one shoots unless I give the order. And if anyone is going to kill this maniac, it's going to be me and I'm going to enjoy it."

Several officers cheered and hooted, but more were unsure of how to react. There was an uncomfortableness in the room and many glanced at the Captain to see his reaction. I wondered if this is normal police banter, but I got the idea it wasn't. I was shocked by his bravado with the Captain was sitting right there; and by the look on his face, the Captain was just as shocked.

The officers began to leave the room by twos and threes, and when it was nearly emptied, the Captain caught Simmons' eye and motioned toward his office. The detective followed but not with his tail between his legs, instead he was metaphorically wagging it.

The door shut and Sparks and I exchanged hopeful looks. Maybe the Captain was finally going to rein in his rogue officer. After a few minutes, we could hear Simmons' voice getting louder and louder. And the Captain raised his voice in response, ending with the Captain yelling, "You won't be anywhere near there on Friday, you're on desk duty until further notice."

The door swung open and Simmons vaulted out and slammed the door hard; he stomped out of the room, with a look on his face that I find hard to describe, but strangely enough I wouldn't call it angry.

Tuesday October 10, 2017

Dear Sam,

The police have gone all out to catch this killer on Friday. They really think that they have outsmarted him. I certainly understand that they would have a presence at the location mentioned in the letter, but they are really putting all their eggs in this one basket or all their power forwards in one defensive zone (boy, I am really struggling with these sports metaphors). Sparks has told me that Simmons has continued to brag about how the police are going to get "the bastard." But he is still on desk duty and will not be participating in the operation afield. Sparks also said that she has talked with the Captain and he has listened to her warning that the killer is probably being misleading, while he agreed, he felt that they still have to pursue this lead. Which, I suppose is the prudent thing to do.

Edmund is still not answering my texts or calls. Sparks assured me that he is still showing up to work, but he is like a reheated French fry (my words not hers, she used the tired cliche of "being a shadow of himself." Nobody enjoys a reheated French fry, it's lost all its French fryiness). I can't help but feel sorry for him, he doesn't have much in his life anymore—no boyfriend, no friends, and failing in the greatest challenge of his life—a one-on-one match of wits with a serial killer, who mocks him every chance he gets. The officers who once held him in esteem, now don't even acknowledge his presence and

Sparks tells me that many of the them openly tease him. I really want to help my puppy—huh, I haven't used that nickname in a while. I've made up my mind, I am going over there tomorrow night and force him to hang out with me. I'm such a good friend.

And, perhaps more importantly, I have the feeling that Gustav is going to pop the question, yes the big question, very soon. I have noticed some subtle clues, he has been asking about my favorite flowers, and I caught him trying to measure the circumference of my ring finger. He thought I was asleep, but I wasn't. He had a string and oh so gently draped around my finger. I think it will be Friday. He is in Chicago right now for business and will return late Thursday night, and so Friday night is the perfect time for a big proposal. He has Friday off work and he will probably take that time to get everything ready. I am mostly definitely going to say a big, ol' gay yes! I love it when all the pieces fall into place.

Wednesday October 11, 2017

Dear Sam,
Oh shit, oh shit, oh shit. What did I do? God, why do I ruin everything? Edmund kissed me, really kissed me and I kind of kissed him back. And more than for a few seconds. But that's it. Oh god. Oh my god!

Last night, I went over to his apartment to hang out with him and I wasn't sure he would even open the door, but he did. We ended going out to dinner at that great Indian place we went to months ago. He was more like his old self, talking random trivia and assuring me he knew best on a wide range of topics. He did steer clear of discussing our friend. It was so good to see him regaining a sense of himself. Then we went back to his place. We were sitting on the couch and he was showing me really boring YouTube videos on sciency stuff on his IPad, then out of nowhere he leaned across and kissed me. Really kissed me. And I kissed him back. Next thing I know, I found that my hands went up under his shirt, feeling his chest. Being this close to him, it just seemed so natural. Then I felt his hand on my leg sliding up to my...at that point, my mind finally took control away from my hormones. I'm I leapt up and made some lame excuse to get out of there. I know I hurt him, but I am completely happy with Gustav...I think. I guess I have some teeny, tiny unresolved feelings for Edmund. Oh god. I have no idea how I'm going to tell Gustav. Or should I even tell Gustav at all? What if he doesn't want to marry me anymore. What if he never wants to speak to me again? I fucked this up, as usual. I knew I would find a way to sabotage this. I am a horrible person. Gustav deserves so much better than me.

Should I text Gustav now? Should I wait until he gets home? I hate all this guilt and anxiety. Why do I constantly ruin my own life?

I just got a text from Edmund, a very uncharacteristically short text, it was one word: Sorry.

Thursday October 12, 2017

I told Gustav this morning. I called him and explained everything. He was not as angry as I thought he would be. He said we would talk tomorrow. He needed the night to himself to think things over. That's fair. He told me he was going back to his hotel room with his roommate from Germany. I can't blame him. I would be furious if our roles were reversed. It's just, we haven't gone this long without communicating. I've gotten used to having his ear, let alone several other more alluring parts of his body. But obviously, I am willing to wait as long as he needs me to. He is worth waiting for.

I hope that this won't ruin our amazing relationship.

Friday October 13, 2017

Dear Sam,
This is my worst nightmare.

Saturday October 14, 2017

Dear Sam,
The events of the past two days keep replaying in my mind. I haven't slept or at least I don't remember sleeping since Thursday morning. I woke up yesterday to no texts, no calls from Gustav. Disappointing, but not too unexpected. I tried to busy myself all morning and hoped that the stakeout in the afternoon would take my mind off things until Gustav contacted me and we can talk through my fiasco. Around noon, with still no word from Gustav, I drove down to the station to hang out with Edmund and Sparks before the stakeout. She was coordinating the efforts from afar. I was not looking forward to seeing Edmund. I knew this would be a super awkward meeting since this was the first contact I had with him since the kissing incident.

I walked in and immediately Edmund came over to me and just stood there sheepishly, not saying a word. I froze for a moment not knowing what to do or say, but then I realized this is Edmund, who is still so new to dating and relationships. He hasn't made connections with many people, except me. (Lyman most definitely does not count). What he did was wrong but understandable and forgivable (I hope Gustav agrees). And if I am honest, I am just as guilty as Edmund in this. I made up my mind then and there that I couldn't abandon my friendship with him, I couldn't do that to him. It is true that I still have feelings for him, romantic, sexual feelings, but I couldn't just abandon him. Friends don't do that. I was hoping that Gustav wouldn't make me choose between a relationship with him or a friendship with Edmund. I would choose Gustav, of course, but I would feel shitty for the rest of my life about Edmund.

I looked at Edmund and said, "Don't say a word. It's ok." And we walked together over to Sparks who was busy doing her police ordering officers around thing.

After a few minutes, she acknowledged our presence. "Hey boys, I'm glad to see you are back to being friends." I'm not sure she knew about the kiss, I know I didn't tell her. But she turned to police matters without questioning anything further. "We have the area well surrounded. If the killer comes anywhere near there, we will get him. But I agree with you Edmund, I don't think he would be this bold, this foolish really. He is probably just laughing at us from miles and miles away. Edmund, what do you his plan is in all this?"

"I am ashamed to say, but I really don't have any idea. Perhaps, he just wants to waste police resources and their time. He has expressed derision for the department in the past," Edmund offered.

Looking about I asked, "Where's the effervescent Detective Simmons? He's not out in the field?"

"No, the Captain absolutely forbade it. He decided to take a personal day since he couldn't get in 'on the action,' as he put it." Sparks replied.

I was glad about that. I found him incredibly irritating. Edmund was condescending and cute, Simmons was condescending and an asshole.

It wasn't long before, the appointed time arrived. Sparks gave us the play by play as the operation proceeded, but ultimately it was a big zero. They stopped a few cars, searched around the area and came up with nothing. The only unusual thing they found was a human skull, but they could tell it was very old. They of course will run tests on it, but nobody thought it was going to be significant. By 4:00, the teams were being recalled, Edmund was chatting with the Captain on the phone, he was asking if the clues could be interpreted any other way. I was just saying my goodbyes to Sparks when my cell rang. It was a number I didn't recognize.

"Hi, Jonathan? This is Imanuel Ehrenhardt, I'm Gustav's work colleague," said a voice with a slight German accent. "I know this is his day off, but he did have some files to email to me, but I haven't heard from him since yesterday morning when he said he was going to be spending the night in our hotel room. He never arrived last night. I assumed he changed his mind and spent the night at your place. I have texted and called, but no answer from him. That is not like him at all. And the strangest thing happened, when I got back to our hotel room from the office, there was a small piece of paper taped to the door."

"What was on the paper?" I barely could get the words out.

"Nothing, but a small red diamond. Weird, no?" He replied.

I dropped the phone, my knees buckled, I collapsed.

Sparks rushed over to me. "My god, Jonathan, are you alright? What's happened?"

I couldn't speak. Sparks picked up my phone and got the story from Imanuel. One of the other officers helped me into a chair and placed a cold cup of water in my hand. I couldn't even think of what to do with it; I had forgotten how to drink. I took one sip and promptly threw up.

Sparks was issuing orders, Edmund was there helping her and googling on his phone, other cops were moving about, making phone calls, but it was all a blur. I was overwhelmed with fear and guilt. I cheated on him and now I will never see him again. This just can't be. I have no one to blame but my own karma.

The next few hours were just a series of isolated moments of lucidity in a stream of blurs. I remember Edmund trying to comfort me in his own Edmundian way. Sparks was in and out and trying to get information out of me like a surgeon removing shrapnel. I don't remember any of her questions or my answers. The next thing I know for sure is that around 3 am, we had gotten into a car. I asked where we are going and Sparks said to find Gustav.

We arrived at an old tavern on the north side of town. It was dark and the parking lot was empty. Edmund hopped out and ran up to the door. He grabbed a piece of paper off of it and returned to the car.

The past leads to the future.

"That's it?" Sparks said incredulously. At the time I didn't notice the strain in her voice. But after thinking about, I now can tell she was ready for this to be over, the constant clues, the puzzles, the people dying were all wearing on her. And of course, this was personal, she knows Gustav and she knows me. "So, where to next?" She prodded Edmund.

Edmund didn't reply for what seemed like many minutes. Finally Sparks called his name in her commanding, but gentle way.

"I was just thinking back to all the killers notes and puzzles, seeing if something could be interpreted differently. The problem is that there are so many clues and they all could have an alternative meaning. Which one is he focusing on? I'm not sure." He explained.

"We never really understood the name of the guy in the last clue...Grisham?" She offered.

"You mean Gershom, yes, it was the name given to Moses' first born. I have thought about that, but I am still drawing a blank on what that could be referring too." He said in response.

"I think you mentioned that it is only used once in all the Bible? Is that right?" She asked.

"No, there are other references, about a half dozen. And you think that one of the verses that mention him might have an additional meaning? Interesting." Edmund mused.

He quickly looked up the first verse, Exodus 2:22: "And she bore him a son, and he called his name Gershom [that is, A stranger there]; for he said, "I have been a stranger in a strange land.""

"Stranger in a Strange Land?" Sparks the sci-fi nerd pondered. "That's the title of a Robert Heinlein novel. Pretty weird stuff if I remember."

"Weird in what way?" Edmund asked.

"It's about an alien who comes to earth and preaches free love and has lots of sex with earth women. Weird, huh?" She replied.

"Yes. But it doesn't immediately trigger anything for me. We are missing something." Edmund said.

"You know, if you think about it, Gustav could be described as a stranger in a strange land." I murmured to myself.

"That's true, that might explain that part of the clue. Or maybe the killer thinks of himself as a stranger in a strange land." Sparks added. "Maybe he is revealing more than he meant to with this reference. Maybe he has revealed a lot more than he meant to with all of his clues."

"I have considered that," Edmund spoke up and in a defeated tone he said, "But I haven't been able to put it all together."

"We know he likes to reference things in music and pop culture and history, but we also know he likes synonyms and word with double meanings," Sparks reminded him. With that Edmund closed his eyes. Even in the very dim light, we could tell he was in deep thought. Sparks and I looked at each other, allowing Edmund some silence.

"I'm just not sure," Edmund said after many minutes. "I have an idea, but it really is just a guess. I am not used to guessing."

"Your guess are better than most people's facts, tell us!" I replied.

"Let's go to Woodland Cemetery?" He said reluctantly.

"What? Why there?" Sparks had asked before I could stop her. Edmund was in a delicate state and didn't really need his ideas questioned right now.

"Several reasons: 1. It is a major city landmark that he hasn't used yet. 2. It is a cemetery, it's outdoors and we know he often likes a public display, and the idea is that being in a cemetery could cause fear in people. 3. It is in a central location in the city and he seems to want to keep to the city limits. 4. It has incredible historical ties to the city through the many famous people interred there. 5. And this is my reason with the least evidence, he wants this to be about death."

For someone who is only guessing, he seems to have really thought this through.

"You convinced me," I said enthusiastically. "Sparks, take us to Woodland Cemetery." Going somewhere felt better than going nowhere. I needed to do something to find Gustav and sitting in Spark's car didn't feel like we were making progress.

She paused in thought for a moment, shrugged her shoulders and then headed that way.

On the drive over, Edmund didn't say much. I could tell he was anxious, more anxious than I had ever seen him. I am sure this situation was weighing on him like the humidity during a Dayton summer. I wondered if this was more worrisome for him because of me, because it is my loved one missing. Is he conflicted here? Could some part of him want Gustav out of the picture so that he can have me all to himself? I was making myself sick thinking about this.

In just a few minutes, we arrived at Woodland Cemetery. The cemetery is old and enormous. It spans more than 200 acres and is the final resting place of more than 100,000 people (last year I went on a ghost tour of the cemetery). We parked by one of the gates, a huge rod-iron construct more than 12 feet tall. It was padlocked, but Sparks, I don't remember how, managed to get us inside.

The cemetery is constructed over several large hills. Sparks picked the nearest one and we began our steep ascent. Despite my enthusiasm before, I was unsure why we were here and what we were looking for.

"Edmund, this place is huge, is there any other clue that might help us narrow our search?" Sparks asked between labored breaths.

Edmund paused as if thinking, but I suspected he was catching his breath—like I was. "Well, two previous clues have dealt with people buried here—the Wright Brothers and Paul Laurence Dunbar. Let me google where they are." I thought this another delay tactic—not that I'm complaining, I've been meaning to get back to the gym, but, you know, things have been a bit busy lately and, somehow, hills seem to have gotten steeper in my old age.

He looked up from his phone and surveyed the area around. It was dark but I did see a tinge of orange creeping into the eastern horizon. Dawn wasn't too far off; as much I was wanting more light for our search, I was equally terrified for what the sun could reveal. Edmund pointed up the hill and we restarted our climb.

We crested the top and saw the memorial to the Wright Brothers. It was meticulously maintained, except for the tacky plastic flowers about it. Why would someone leave cheap, plastic flowers? Not noticing anything unusual or any clue, we cast about for Dunbar's headstone.

We located it quickly and a cursory search revealed nothing. Edmund exhaled deeply through his nose, it was one of his few expressions of emotion.

"If we split up we can cover more ground," Edmund suggested. This was not a good idea, in my humble opinion. Walking around alone in one of the most haunted cemeteries in the Midwest while a crazy killer could be laying in wait is not my idea of a genius plan.

Surprisingly Sparks agreed and we each wandered off in our own direction. The mid October night air was cold, I rubbed my arms to maintain some warmth. I shifted uncomfortably from foot to foot. I tried not to think about what the end of this ludicrous chase might reveal. What is Gustav going through? How is he being tortured? Is he already dead? How will we ever find him? I stopped and leaned against a large tombstone. In that moment of quiet, all the emotions of the last few months burst forth. The tears came, the tears of frustration, of grief, of fear and of helplessness, of hope and of despair. My chest heaved in uncontrollable sobs; I couldn't stop, not for a long time.

I don't think I have ever loved anyone so fully, so overwhelmingly as Gustav, not even you Sam—please forgive me for saying this. And what of Edmund? He is trying so hard to help me, even if he feels some jealousy toward Gustav; he is still trying. I looked in his direction and realized something, something I have been scared to admit, I love him too. Is it I want to marry you and have your children kind of love? I'm not sure. But it is more than let's hang out some weekend and play Ticket to Ride kind of love. I want Edmund in my life and I want Gustav in my life.

I immediately chastised myself. Here, Gustav's life is in danger and I am greedily wanting the love of two men. I am a terrible human being. At that moment, I felt cold, alone and absolutely wretched and the tears were still coming. I foolishly tried to hide my tears, but in this darkness no one could see them anyway. For some reason, my thoughts then went to all the dead that lay around me and the people that the killer had murdered. These people were torn from their lives. These people lived and loved, had joy and sorrow. But now no more. They are worm food—ugh, I am referencing Shakespeare, I have indeed sunk low. Are the dead satisfied with the life that was given them? Do they have regrets? Did they pass by opportunity because of fear or because of waiting for something better? Or did they settle for what was convenient? Henry David Thoreau said, "Most men lead lives of quiet desperation." Is that me? I hope not.

C.S. Lewis once wrote, "Crying is all right in its way while it lasts. But you have to stop sooner or later and then you still have to decide what to do." I had always thought that he was a bit callous for writing this, but I do see some wisdom in it. I could stay there feeling sorry for myself, the murdered and all those souls about me, but it doesn't help solve the problem at hand. Of course, the emotional impact of this must be dealt with eventually, but I needed to do something now and wandering blindly through this cemetery was not it. I stood on my feet and walked back in the direction of Edmund and Sparks. After that release of raw emotion, I think I had gained some clarity: we can't waste our time here. We have to decipher the clues we have and stop this madman and rescue Gustav and I have to mend my relationship with him and figure out a way to get him to marry me...ok, let's slow down, one step at a time.

I called out for Sparks and Edmund. They both were eager in asking if I found anything.

"No, but we are wasting our time here. We can't just wander around this place hoping to stumble upon the killer. Edmund, I know that you said you were stumped. But we can try to figure out something from the killer's last clue." I said with as much hope as I could muster.

A deep stillness settled between us. I saw, or imagined I saw, a depth of sadness in his eye that I don't think I have ever seen before in anyone. Eventually, Edmund broke the silence, in what I could only describe as a selfless act of humility, and asked Sparks if we should call in Detective Simmons since he had had some success against the killer.

"I mean, I guess. You're right he has been helpful with this in the past. I am still mystified how he solved those puzzles. Where did he get such acumen?" Sparks replied shaking her head in disbelief.

"Acumen, what a funny word. I remember where I first learned that word," I said aloud reminiscing, "it was in a song by REM and I distinctly remember having to look it up in dictionary. That was a great CD."

"I love REM, but I don't remember a song with the word "acumen" in it. Was it on <u>Automatic for the People</u>?" She replied.

"No, it was on <u>Document</u>."

"Which song?"

"Um...'Exhuming McCarthy', I think."

"What other songs were on that CD?"

"Um, 'the Finest Work Song,' 'The One I love,' and 'It's the End of the World as I Know it (and I feel fine).'" I rattled off.

"That is a great song," Sparks mused.

"There was one more that wasn't as popular but I really loved, 'King of Birds.'" I stated.

Sparks and I were silently listening to the songs in our heads when Edmund froze.

"One of the songs was called 'King of Birds?'"

"Yes." Sparks and I said in unison.

"One of the translations of the name the killer has signed his letters with, Tarkshya, is the king of birds. Perhaps this isn't a coincidence." This was as excited as I have ever seen Edmund get.

All over us pulled up the lyrics on our phones.

"Standing on the shoulders of giants, leaves me cold," I read.

"A mean idea to call my own," Sparks continued.

"I am the king of all I see, my kingdom for a voice." Edmund finished.

The killer had used all these phrases in his letters and clues. But I couldn't see what it told us other than he was an REM fan. Sparks and I sat there waiting for Edmund to speak. We all felt that this was the clue to unraveling the whole mystery. It had such portent, such weight. This was the final piece—Edmund just had to place it in its right spot.

But Edmund sat staring off at nothing. His lips formed words without sound, his hands twitched and his head moved slowly from side to side. Sweat began to form on his brow, despite the chilly October air. His eyes narrowed in concentration. Edmund gritted his teeth, doing all he could to increase his concentration. His breath quickened and then became more shallow. He even rocked a little back and forth.

Soon he began walking aimlessly about. A few feeble rays of light peaked over the horizon. But they only revealed a frantic, unhinged, desperate man. His hands moved in a repetitive motion, making circles for a moment until he realized what he was doing and drop them by his sides, only to have them start up again without realizing it, almost as if he was having an unconscious twitch.

After a long pause, Edmund said, "I'm sorry Jonathan, I don't think I can solve this riddle. I have no idea where Gustav is, I have failed you. The killer has beaten me at my own game."

My heart broke. The killer had robbed Edmund of his very identity and left him a man in doubt of himself. I tried to find words to comfort him, but I had no fortitude to do so. I had nothing to give him but what I felt were empty words.

"Edmund, you haven't failed me. You solved puzzles and riddles that no one else could. You weren't trained to handle serial killers. He hasn't beaten you at your own game, you were trained to be a forensic accountant." I said.

Somewhere in my brain a long unused neuron fired.

"You are a forensic accountant," I said excitedly. "Edmund, we have been going about this all wrong. We haven't let you do what you are best at. We have been pushing you to decipher Uber-cryptic messages, which you have done better than anyone, but that's not your strength. I remember how you described your job to me when we first met. You said that you look at patterns, find discrepancies and analyze their meaning. That's your strength. Do that."

Edmund looked stunned.

"This killer isn't an excel file about some embezzled money, this is a psychopathic murderer," Sparks pointed out.

"The principle is the same. You have data, the killer's notes and actions, find the patterns and then find the discrepancies and analyze them. Do *your* job!" I replied.

Edmund was silent. Weighing my words, he paused, then gave a brief nod. He began thinking. Thinking, what about, I couldn't be sure. He sat down on a low tombstone and sat and nothing more. After a while, he stood up and began again in earnest. In a similar way as before but infinitely different, he began to move his hands in the air making invisible columns and adding in invisible data. His body language was so markedly different from a just a few minutes ago that I almost could imagine that he was a different person. A narrowing of his eyes, a tilt of his head (still cute), and a wry smile crept across his lips. Then I saw it, in his eyes, the search of the data, the connections being made, the finding of the discrepancies and lastly, the conclusion of his analysis.

"His last clue said, 'The past will lead to the future.'" More to himself than us. "He has a pattern, a shockingly regular pattern. And then there is the discrepancy. I know where he is, more accurately, where he will be."

He waited. Was he pausing for dramatic effect? Edmund, what the hell, tell us!

Sparks' impatience got the best of her, "Damn it, Edmund, talk." She barked.

"His whole motivation for his crimes has been to prove to others that he is superior. The King of Birds song reveals much about his psyche. He wants to be original and for other people to recognize his genius. He is willing to trade everything in his life for, as the song puts it, my kingdom for a voice. He has been overlooked his whole life and now, with these murders, he has changed that. Furthermore, he also wants revenge against everyone who has overlooked him, in essence the whole city. Which means Dayton is his home town, but we already guessed that. We all know he has confined his crimes almost entirely to within the city limits. Most criminals know that committing crimes in different jurisdictions helps them. Different police departments often do not work well together, but he is making it more difficult on himself by confining his crime to only Dayton proper. Why? Because he is taking his revenge on this city. He has been holding the city hostage for months. He wants to prove definitively he is not standing on the shoulders of giants, he is the true genius, he is better than everyone."

"Were there any times he broke his pattern?" I asked.

"Yes, obviously. And that has told me so much. What was the only incident to take place outside of the city limits?" He asked with professorial air.

"Oh my god, when he tried to kill Gustav and me at the Bed and Breakfast in Springboro!' I exclaimed.

"Yes, and what does that tell us?" Edmund replied.

"That he hates B&Bs?" I tried. "No, wait, that he wanted to kill me?"

"No, on both counts, what it tell us is that his target was Gustav." Edmund countered. And then paused for effect. But it was lost on both Sparks and me.

"He is escalating this. If he kills, especially publicly kills, a foreign national, his fame will go around the world. And Dayton's reputation will sink even lower. And that is what he really wants. His past crimes haven't really been public, yes, someone would eventually stumble across the body, but this killing, his killing of Gustav will be before a live audience. This event, this crime will be at the very center of the city, so the whole city can see. Eliminating all the other possibilities, there are no major sporting events tonight, no festivals, so the only place that people will be out and about tonight will be at Riverscape. And it will be tonight. The weather is good. This will be his showcase killing; he feels he will get revenge on the city that has wronged him and he will make the world recognize his genius."

"And the icing on the cake is defeating you," Sparks added.

What a weird paradox of emotions that ran through me. Elation at finally cracking this killer's code and utter despair that Gustav could be tortured and killed.

"So, what do we do?" I asked Sparks and Edmund.

"That's a good question. I'm not sure how the Captain will want to handle this: discreet with plain clothes officers mingled into the crowd or an overwhelming police presence to protect the public." Sparks replied.

"Do we have to tell him? I am not feeling particularly disposed to him. And if we do, then I think we should only tell the Captain. If this becomes common knowledge, I'm afraid he will kill Gustav and try again with a different plan" I said, expressing my lack of confidence in the police and their methods.

"I'm definitely going to tell him. If I go rogue on this one, I will probably lose my job and perhaps get jail time, let alone risk Gustav's life and others as well. I have to tell him." Sparks said firmly.

We left the cemetery as the sunrise filled the grounds with light and a little bit of warmth. I could have really gone for some high end breakfast tea and a bear claw from Bill's Donuts.

When we arrived at the station, things were quiet. The Captain wasn't there yet, Sparks had called him on the way over, but we beat him there. Once inside it was clear that a dejected feeling hung in the air among the officers. They had worked so hard, but without any real results. But thanks to Edmund that could change.

Sparks started in on her thing, but there wasn't much for us to do until the captain arrived; however, I desperately needed to do something. Sitting still doesn't really work for me at the best of times and this was definitely not the best of times. I went in search of something to keep my mind and hands busy. Edmund followed me like the proverbial lost puppy. I eventually found the break room at the station, and made myself and Edmund some tea, just a generic black tea blend. There were no bear claws, but we found a couple of slices of pizza left over from the night before. I definitely felt like a college kid again, having cold pizza and cheap tea for breakfast.

Edmund and I chewed our pizza in silence. During this time, I had surges of guilt that I am eating and drinking while Gustav could be out there dying. I tried to reassure myself that I was doing all I could to find him. Part of me wanted to drive around the city shouting his name, but my mind told my nerves that the best hope of helping Gustav was to stay near to Edmund. It didn't help. After half a slice I couldn't eat any more.

All through my internal guilt struggle, Edmund had been thoughtfully chewing, content in the silence, staring at nothing. He ate three slices and drank two cups of tea. I watched him with a bit of a side eye, wondering what was going on his eclectic brain. What was he feeling? Anxiety? Calm? Was still analyzing data? Was he reveling in his victory? Did he still feel guilt?

"For cold pizza, this is pretty good," he said quietly. Well, that was anti-climatic.
At that moment, Sparks stuck her head in and beckoned us to follow, leading us to the Captain's office. He looked remarkable well put together for a man awoken at an ungodly hour and called into work on a Saturday. A burnt orange polo and some khakis, snaps for the Captain dressing in seasonal colors.

He asked us to sit down and what followed was a long discussion about what we had uncovered and what it meant. He asked many, many questions that really plumbed the depths of Edmund's reasoning, his deductions and his motives. Though never rude or accusatory, the Captain asked some really hard questions. I think he still had Simmon's bug in his ear that Edmund might be more involved than he was letting on.

Every time I moved to speak to defend Edmund, Sparks put her had on my arm, letting me know that now was not the time. At that moment, I both loved and hated her.

After more than an hour and a half of this, the Captain rubbed his eyes a bit and asked Edmund and I to step out. I think Sparks had to undergo her own inquisition from the Captain. We returned to the break room where I made more tea.

Forty or so minutes later Sparks returned. She wasn't exactly smiling, but she seemed optimistic. She told that us the Captain believed Edmund's reasoning was solid and had come up with a plan, he had opted for a more covert operation than a show of force. He had dispatched some officers to go through the park now and throughout the day. In the evening, he was going to place plain clothes officers all about the park and felt confident that this would give us the best chance of catching this lunatic.

"There's one more thing. And you probably aren't going to like it: the Captain wants you two to be in police custody until tonight." She paused gauging our reaction. "But it isn't too bad, he said I could look after you. So, gents, it is off to my place, where you can clean up and we'll order some food."

I was pissed at this. The Captain doesn't trust us, after all we have been through. I felt like telling him off and refusing to comply. But the alternative was probably me being arrested and in locked in a jail cell. And we all know that I am too pretty for prison.

I spent the day not sleeping, even though I was tired as hell. I did manage a few sporadic moments of rest, for a grand total of 45 minutes. Around 5 pm, Sparks had some food delivered but it tasted like ash, probably because of the gut wrenching anxiety, but it might have been Spark's choice of a discount restaurant—she had a coupon, eye roll emoji goes here. Around 6pm, Sparks announced that we could go and watch the operation from a discreet distance. I was so surprised that you could have knocked me over with a spork.

"The Captain wants you nearby in case we need Edmund's expertise," She explained.

"And probably to keep on eye on me," Edmund said without a hint of bitterness. How could he not be bitter? The Captain was treating him like a common criminal. Why wasn't he furious? I was furious that he was not furious. He seemed utterly unfazed by his treatment from the Captain. I would have stewed all day over it, not Edmund though, he spent the day peacefully sleeping, how is that even possible? All afternoon, I wandered from room to room in Sparks' tiny, shabby, sparsely decorated house. If any ever needed a gay best friend, it was her.

A half hour before sunset, we loaded up in her car and made the short trip downtown. We parked close to the minor league ball park, Fifth-Third Field—home of the Dragons! Go Sports! Sparks led us to the back of a PNC bank building that overlooked the park.

"The owner of this building is a big supporter of the department and allows us access for operations from time to time. In return, we let him sit in on some minor stake outs," She explained as she unlocked a back door and took us up to the roof in a freight elevator.

"Remember the rules, don't stand up, especially at the edge of the building, it will look suspicious. Don't make a lot of noise. Don't offer suggestions, Edmund, unless the officers here ask you. We will be working with Henry Wilmans and Knolt Hoheimer, you've worked with them before." He nodded in recognition. The doors of the freight elevator noisily opened and we walked onto the roof. It was warmer than last night, a perfect fall evening, the kind that lends itself to a walk in a park, I write this with more than a hint of irony. Over in a corner two officers were seated against the parapet. One was holding binoculars and scanning the park. The other crept toward us and gave a quick update.

"No sign of any one suspicious. There's more foot traffic than I would have thought, but I guess people are out enjoying the weather, before it changes." He explained.

At that moment, his radio crackled. "Suspicious activity at Fifth-Third Field plaza."

That was behind us and away from the park. Sparks and the two other officers repositioned themselves on the other side of the roof. We could see them talking hurriedly and subtly pointing.

Some far away pops could be heard at that moment from the total opposite direction of Fifth-Third plaza. Then the radio came to life, "Shots fired near the corner of Jefferson and Monument. Officer in trouble." The officers heads snapped in the other direction. That intersection is on the far end of the park, several blocks away from us. Edmund stood up, but I yanked him down, not wanting the killer to spot us—and not to get yelled at by Sparks and possibly lose our viewing privileges.

And then at that moment, screams rippled through the crowd in the park, people began running. It didn't sound like screams of terror, it sounded more of excitement. I really wanted to know what was going on. I wildly gesticulated to Sparks. The officers moved back to their original location and scanned the park with their binoculars.

"It looks like a fight has broken out. It's hard to tell. People seem to be pushing each other. They are stooped over, picking something up off the ground." Then he added mystified. "I think they are picking up money, dollar bills."

What the hell was going on?

The radio came on again. "Wilmans and Hoheimer, investigate the suspicious figure at Fifth/Third." The two officers looked at each other in surprise, but then handed the binoculars off to Sparks and made their way down.

The radio sputtered again, dispatching various officers to other locations. I had a sinking feeling. This didn't seem right. Even I, who is not always the brightest color in the rainbow, realized that they officers were being called from their locations in and around the park and sent off to other parts of the city.

Edmund crouch-walked to the edge and looked out over the park. The park itself ran along the southern bank of the Great Miami River. The Riverside bridge spanned the Great Miami, forming the eastern edge of the park. Stationed just east of the bridge was one was of six water cannons that the city had purchased in 2001. They were metal towers 60 feet tall set on large concrete bases. They looked a bit like radio towers. These cannons could spray water a couple of hundred feet in the air and the bases held colored lights to make some pretty awesome effects. A few people said that the cost was in the millions for these, I hope not. They are nice, but they just spray water and shine lights, even if they are pretty cool to watch. To be honest, I've never really paid them much attention before. They were just coming on as the sun was setting. One cannon shot a stream a hundred feet into air and colored lights light it up like a very wet firework. Then another cannon went off. Then two in unison, then all six. Maybe it was worth what they cost. Except, every now and then, if the breeze was just right, a faint spray of water would reach us. Good thing it was getting dark and no one could see what all this moisture was doing to my hair.

Sparks had already moved to join Edmund at the edge and I followed suit. The three of us looked out, we saw the chaos in the park, the throng of people had grown rather than diminished. There were only one or two officers in the park trying to control the maddening crowds, but without much success.

All of a sudden, a flood light came on and illuminated the water cannon nearest us. Not so much the cannon itself but the tower around it. And for the first time, I noticed that it had a black tarp wrapped around part of its framework. I looked about at the other cannons' towers and none of them had a similar tarp. And then, as I was staring right at it, the tarp dropped. Tied to the interior of the tower, lashed to its metal framework was a person. From this distance I couldn't make out much of the figure, but I really had no doubt—it was Gustav. The person's head was sunk upon its chest and did not move at all. Oh my god—he was dead. I turned away, I couldn't bear to see him like that.

An earsplitting scream of sheer torture stole the air from my lungs. The screaming continued and forced my attention back to the tower. I saw that the figure was screaming in agony. He wasn't dead, but being tortured. I could tell, even from this distance, that his body writhed in pain, from what I couldn't be sure. The sounds from the park diminished as the people turned to watch the figure squirming under the torture.

I began to panic and run about like an idiot. I was saying something but I can't remember exactly what. Sparks was trying to calm me down, but with little effect. The next thing I knew, I was laying on the roof, my face and hands, scraped and painful.

"I'm sorry I had to trip you, but your panicking is not helpful," Edmund said without much empathy.

Thanks—I think. A slap across the face is more traditional and leaves less scarring I thought as I cleaned tiny pebbles out of my palms.

"Let's go!" Sparks said in her commander voice and we headed towards the elevator. She was on the radio relaying information about the situation and calling for the EMTs. The replies were surprisingly few.

We went out the back door and rounded the corner of the building. Right in front of us, there was a slope down to the river and right there on the bank was the water cannon tower that held Gustav. As we headed toward the slope, we head a voice bark, "Stop."

We turned and saw it was Simmons, wearing his stupid frumpy trench coat. "Sparks, have you forgotten all your training? You can't put yourself in harm's way to futilely attempt to rescue a Vic. And you can't at all bring these civilians into a possible line of fire. We can't lose our heads about this or there will be more casualties."

Sparks paused, getting control of her emotions. "You're right, Walter. Maybe my objectivity isn't as clear as it should be. All right, we wait for back up." She conceded.

"No, my husband is dying out there at I'm going to help him if I can," I ejaculated.

"Husband?" "When did you get married?" "Like hell, he is your husband." The three of them said at the same time.

That's what they focused on? Not the fact that Gustav was being tortured.

"It doesn't matter. I'm going." I said again.

Sparks grabbed me by the collar. "Jonathan, if the killer shoots you, you won't be able to help him. It is likely that he is using Gustav as bait, to draw us out into the open. We have to stay here and wait for back up. I know this is hard, but we can't risk anymore lives." I could hear both sternness and compassion in her voice. Damn it, Sparks, you and your voice of reason. But as Gustav's screams continued, I felt torn between reason and wanting to save the man I loved. But I did heed Sparks' warning and reasoning; thus we waited helplessly for what seemed an eternity, and we waited in silence. The water and light show illuminated our dark situation—ironic, huh? Sparks had her hand on my shoulder in a comforting and in a controlling way. Edmund stared out at Gustav, I had not a clue what was going on is his head—probably still thinking about how good that cold pizza was. Sorry, that was me being a bit salty.

Another scream erupted from Gustav. We turned to watch him flail in his excruciation. I moved to help him but Sparks held me back again. Then several things happened at once. I heard Sparks yell "what the hell" and ungracefully crumple to ground. Next, I felt something tear into my left shoulder, bringing with it such pain as I have never felt or even imagined before, I collapsed to the ground and rolled onto my right side. As I turned my head, I saw Simmons standing there with a syringe in his right hand and his gun in his left.

"I'm a good shot even with my left hand," Simmons gloated and turned to look at Edmund. "Now, this is how it should be. Just you and me," he said. Edmund had instinctively put his hands up and began backing away from Simmons.

Simmons dropped the syringe, switched his gun to his right hand and moved to follow Edmund. Talking all the while. I don't remember much of what he said. I was a little distracted by the searing pain of a gun shot wound in my shoulder, and the agonized cries of Gustav.

Soon they were out of my sight. I had to do something. I crawled over to Sparks and determined she was still breathing but completely unconscious. I tried to get her gun, but she was laying on it and I didn't have the arm strength to move her. Putting my right shoulder against the building I somehow managed to stand. I was a bit woozy and stumbled a bit, but I was determine to help Gustav and Edmund. I followed them out to the street. Edmund was slowly backing up across the bridge, Simmons had his back to me while he pursued Edmund. And he kept up his rant.

"All right Edmund, stop moving or I will kill the German," Simmons holding up what looked like a small TV remote. I saw him press a button and Gustav screamed. They were about a third of the way across the bridge, just about even with the water tower.

Edmund stopped. I moved closer as quietly as I could. The pain had lessened but I knew I had lost a good amount of blood. But I was determined to do something. At least now, I was close enough to hear their conversation.

"You can't get away with this forever, you will be caught," Edmund said in such a weirdly calm voice.

"Are you crazy? Of course, I am going to get away with this. I have thought of everything. I've planned out this with such care. Even you will concede now that I am a genius. The other officers are scurrying around the city on false calls, and no one will be able to identify me. I could have killed you all back there, but what's the fun in that. I want to play a while longer with you. But have no doubt, I will kill you. The police will find all your bodies and hear me tell how I tried to stop the killer, but he got to you first. They will say it was a tragedy, but my heroic actions saved more live. I might even get a medal."

I was slowly, so slowly advancing on Simmons. To his credit, never once did Edmund look at me but kept his eyes focused on Simmons. But curiously every now and then, he did glance at his watch. What was he waiting for, a bus?

"One thing I never figured out was where you obtained the Rocuronium Bromide." Edmund stated flatly.

"I can't believe that's the only thing you haven't figured out, but you should have. I stole the Bromide from the Tuscan Police department evidence room. I worked for them a few years back. It was so easy. No one ever suspected anything, I had them all fooled. Just like I have the Dayton police fooled. It was so entertaining to have the force running around trying to figure out my clues." Simmons paused, his face becoming more serious. "Have you ever seen someone die? It is really interesting. I'm going to let you watch the German die, and then it is your turn." Simmons threatened as he held the remote aloft. Edmund glanced at his watch again and Simmons noticed it, puzzled.

At that moment, a big spray of water from the water cannon soaked us all, it was shockingly cold and made my wound ache all over again, I managed to stifle a gasp of pain. Simmons was shaking the water off. I guess that was Edmund's plan all along, maneuvering Simmons to this spot on the bridge, but I am not sure if it did any good.   Then I noticed that Simmons had dropped the remote into the darkness.

"Your little trick didn't do much. It will only delay the inevitable. A wet gun will still work, you should know that." Simmons sneered.

"Jonathan now!" Edmund screamed catching me completely off guard. Simmons swung around and fired, but this time his aim was off and the bullet pierced my right leg and hurt almost as bad as the first time I was shot that night. There's a something I never thought I would experience, being shot twice in the same night. I collapsed to the ground, screaming what I like to imagine was a very manly scream. I was in too much pain in the moment to realize that Edmund's plan had failed. I wasn't able to do anything to stop Simmons. Hope ebbed from me quicker than my blood. Then I heard something like someone falling to the ground.

Shaking the water out of my eyes, I looked up to see Edmund standing over Simmons with a stun gun, wires from the gun connecting the two. "A stun gun will work as well while wet. I researched it." As I faded into unconsciousness, I thought that for his first attempt at snarkiness, it wasn't that bad.

Epilogue

Saturday October 28, 2017

Dear Sam,
Gustav and I leave for Germany tomorrow morning. After his ordeal, he wanted to spend some time at home, his home, and he asked me to go with him. His company has been great, offering him quite a few paid weeks of time off to help him with his recovery. And I can work from anywhere with WiFi. We'll be staying with his mother for a while, but he also has been talking about renting a small flat just for us. I suggested a Bavarian castle, but he just smiled. Nevertheless, I am really excited about this.

Both Gustav and I healed up all right, at least physically. I was in the hospital much longer than he was. He had several electrical burns on his body, I tell him it adds to his already sparking personality. Sparks recovered in about two hours. She had no lasting effects from the Rocuronium Bromide. I know we both have a long way to go before we can say that we "have dealt with this." We both feel it would be a good idea to find a therapist to work with either over there or when we get back here or both. We have talked about Edmund and my kiss, he has forgiven me, but I know I still have a lot work to do to mend the rift I caused in our relationship. I am just happy that he is giving me the chance to do so.

The police want us back in town for Simmons' trial but that won't be for months and months, maybe even more than a year. For what Sparks has told me, Simmons has been uncooperative to say the least. He had lawyered up immediately, but Sparks wasn't too worried. On top of our testimony, there was a pile of physical evidence found at his house that will put him away for the rest of his life.

Everything was ready for our move overseas, but I had one last errand to do before escaping to Europe.

I went to see Edmund one more time. He asked me to meet him out at Cox Arboretum. I exited the parking lot and walked right to the turtle pond. Although it was late October, the evening was still warm in the half hour before sunset. The trees had lost most of their leaves and the sun shone through the emptying branches. I found Edmund on the little bridge spanning the pond with his arms resting on the rails and his chin upon his arms. He didn't look up as I approached.

"You leave in the morning?" He said breaking the silence.

"Yes, it's a long flight, about 10 hours," I replied.

"Are you really sure you want to go?" He asked.

"Oh yes, I think it will good for both of us...both Gustav and I," I clarified.

Edmund made no reply.

"Have you gone back to work?" I asked.

"No, not for the police, not yet," he stated. "I have some private clients who have provided me with a fair amount of work. To be honest, I have been sleeping a lot, like ten, eleven hours a night."

"I think that's ok," I said. "Sleep can help you recuperate."

He shrugged his shoulders and lapsed into silence, staring at the remaining couple of turtles still basking in the last few rays of the sun.

I looked at him. "He was man, taking all for all..." Here, Shakespeare seemed appropriate. I think I have finally unraveled my mixed up feelings for him. I do love him, with all his quirks and perks. But I no longer desire him, no longer want any romantics from him. He is my friend. Such a common word for having survived horrors together, he is more than a friend. We have shared the same suffering, we have fought the evil in the world, and though victorious, we are not unscathed. There should be a word for a person who has gone through the same terrible events with you and survived. Despite having nearly half a million words, sometimes the English language is just so incomplete.

I still thought of Edmund as a puppy, just not my puppy, I no longer can claim any ownership over him. I still want him to be taken care, I want him to be fed and comfortable, loved and comforted, but I can no longer be the one who provides that. For my well-being and his, I am letting him go—but I will always be his friend.

Edmund was facing away from the setting sun, but I was watching its slow descent, my hands resting behind me on the rail, when suddenly I felt Edmund take my hand in his. I looked down at our hands, then up to his face, etched with uncharacteristic sorrow and pleading.

"Please, don't go, I need you," Edmund whispered.

Oh boy.

The end.

About the author: J. K. Zimmerman is a quiet, mild-mannered man with an overactive imagination and some free time on his hands. When not imagining a world of serial killers and sassy gays, he likes to do woodworking and gardening; he also enjoys gaming with his weekly game group. He lives with his husband and dog, Basil, in the town of Dayton, Ohio.

Made in the USA
Monee, IL
03 December 2021

83841936R00087